Stage
Fright

Christy® Fiction Series

Christy® Fiction Series

Stage Fright

Catherine Marshall
adapted by C. Archer

Thomas Nelson, Inc.
Nashville • London • Vancouver

STAGE FRIGHT
Book Ten in the *Christy*® Fiction Series

Copyright © 1997
by the Estate of Catherine Marshall LeSourd

The *Christy*® Fiction Series is based on *Christy*®
by Catherine Marshall LeSourd © 1967
by Catherine Marshall LeSourd

The *Christy*® name and logo are officially registered
trademarks of the Estate of Catherine Marshall LeSourd

Managing Editor: Laura Minchew
Project Editor: Beverly Phillips

Library of Congress Cataloging-in-Publication Data

Archer, C. 1956–
    Stage fright / Catherine Marshall ; adapted by C. Archer.
        p.   cm. — (Christy fiction series ; 10)
    Summary: After Christy's students at the mission school in Cutter
Gap put on a play, circumstances lead Christy to follow her own
dream of acting, but mysterious incidents threaten to mar her stage
debut.
    ISBN 0-8499-3961-5 (pbk.)
    [1. Theater—Fiction. 2. Teachers—Fiction. 3. Mountain life—
Fiction. 4. Christian life—Fiction.] I. Marshall, Catherine, 1914–
1983. II. Title. III. Series : Archer, C., 1956– Christy fiction
series ; 10.
PZ8.3.W42455Wh   1996
[Fic]—dc21

                                                              96-45388
                                                                   CIP
                                                                    AC

Printed in the United States of America

97 98 99 00 OPM 9 8 7 6 5 4 3 2 1

The Characters

CHRISTY RUDD HUDDLESTON, a nineteen-year-old schoolteacher in Cutter Gap.

CHRISTY'S STUDENTS:
    CREED ALLEN, age nine.
    LITTLE BURL ALLEN, age six.
    BESSIE COBURN, age twelve.
    LIZETTE HOLCOMBE, age fifteen.
    MOUNTIE O'TEALE, age ten.
    RUBY MAE MORRISON, age thirteen.
    MABEL, age eight.

DAVID GRANTLAND, the young minister.
IDA GRANTLAND, David's sister and the mission housekeeper.

ALICE HENDERSON, a Quaker missionary who helped start the mission at Cutter Gap.

DR. NEIL MACNEILL, the physician of the Cove.
MRS. CORA GRAY, the doctor's aunt from Knoxville.
ROBERT GRAY, deceased husband of Cora.

JOSEPH MCPRATT, JR., the boy who starred with Christy in a high school production of *Romeo and Juliet*.

JEB SPENCER, Cutter Gap's finest dulcimer player.

PETER MULBERRY, friend of Dr. MacNeill during medical school.

JAMES BRILEY, former medical school classmate of Dr. MacNeill.

MEMBERS OF THE KNOXVILLE PLAYERS:
    ARABELLA DEVAINE, costume and set designer.
    OLIVER FLUMP, assistant director.
    GILROY GANNON, actor.
    MARYLOU MARSH, Arabella's assistant.
    VERNON MARSH, Marylou's brother.
    SARAH MCGEORGE, actress.
    PANSY TROTMAN, understudy.

MABEL, one of the schoolhouse's resident hogs.

❧ One ❧

Has anyone seen Goldilocks?" Christy Huddleston called as she surveyed her crowded schoolroom.

With seventy students in one room, things were always a little disorganized. Today, however, the room was in chaos.

Of course, it was a very special day. Today was the dress rehearsal of the school's first play, *Goldilocks and the Three Bears.*

Christy climbed onto her desk and clapped her hands. "Attention, everyone!" A few students paused. Christy tried again. "Children!" she called, trying to make herself heard over the babble of excited voices. "What did I tell you about the director of a play?"

"The director gets to boss everybody else around," answered Creed Allen. Creed, who was nine, had been cast in the role of the father bear, or, as the children called him, "Pa Bear."

He paused to adjust the beaver pelt that comprised his costume. Christy had helped Creed tie it around his head with a piece of string. He didn't look anything like a bear, of course, but that didn't matter. As Christy had been teaching them all month, the theater was about make-believe.

Teaching at the mission school here in Cutter Gap always meant working without the usual supplies. But by now, Christy had grown skilled at making do with very little. In fact, she'd chosen the story of the three bears because it required so few props. Christy had written the simple play herself.

Gazing around the room, she felt certain that the schoolhouse was going to work nicely as a theater. (It already served as the church on Sundays.) Christy had talked Miss Ida, who ran the mission house, into parting with a worn sheet.

David Grantland, the young minister for the Cutter Gap mission and Miss Ida's brother, had strung a rope across part of the room. With a little ingenuity, Christy had a curtain for her makeshift stage.

"All right. I see my three bears," Christy called loudly.

"Six bears, Teacher," said Ruby Mae Morrison. Thirteen-year-old Ruby Mae had been wearing her bear costume for days now. The costume was really nothing more than a huge brown coat, far too large for Ruby Mae. She'd found the coat in a box of clothes donated to the mission by a church in Christy's hometown. Christy was allowing Ruby Mae to use it for the play, as long as she promised to return it to the box in good shape.

"Ain't but just three bears in the play," said Bessie Coburn, one of Ruby Mae's best friends. "You all is just underbears."

"Understudies, Bessie," Christy corrected.

"We's proper bears!" Ruby Mae exclaimed. She growled menacingly and clawed at the air, just the way Christy had instructed during "bear lessons" yesterday. "We's the ones who'll take your place if'n somebody eats you up, Ma Bear!"

Bessie sighed as she adjusted her bear costume. "I still don't see why we have to do such a babyish play."

"I wanted to do a play with a plot that even the youngest children could understand, Bessie," Christy explained. "If this first play goes well, maybe we can try something more complicated next time." She smiled. "Who knows? We could even stage a play by Shakespeare."

"Shakespeare?" Bessie repeated.

"He was a very fine writer who lived a long time ago," Christy replied. "In the meantime, I want you to be the very best bear you can possibly be, all right?"

While Bessie and Ruby Mae engaged in a mock bear fight, Christy once again clapped her hands. "Let's everyone take our places for the final scene," she called.

Finally, everyone paid attention. Christy watched in delight as the children rushed to their places. In all her months of teaching, she'd never seen them so excited about a project.

When she'd told Miss Alice Henderson, the Quaker missionary who'd helped start the mission school, about her plan to stage a play, Miss Alice had shaken her head. "Are you sure you're not biting off more than you can chew, Christy?" she'd asked. "After all, you've only been teaching a short time. Maybe you should save such a big production for next year."

"But I loved the theater when I was going to school," Christy had replied. "I know the children will love it, too."

And they had. She'd somehow found a way to give each child an important part to play, even if it wasn't on stage. They'd built simple sets. They'd learned about how to behave in the audience. And they'd even learned a little bit about acting.

"Places, everyone!" Christy called. "Is Goldilocks in position?"

"Yes'm, Miz Christy," Creed said, grinning. He pointed to the smallest bed, where a figure lay covered by a threadbare sheet.

Christy had decided that Lizette Holcombe should play Goldilocks, but it had been a controversial casting choice. Because Lizette had brown hair, many of the other students had objected. But Lizette had a real presence on stage. Besides, she was one of the few students in class who could memorize all the lines.

"Little Burl, the curtain!" Christy called.

Little Burl Allen pulled back the sheet that separated the desks and benches from the stage area.

"Pa Bear," Christy whispered loudly. "Your line!"

Creed cleared his throat. He lumbered toward the first bed. The bed was made of a few crude boards that the older students had nailed together with David's help.

Creed yanked on the worn sheet covering the bed. "I declare!" he cried. "Somebody's been a-sleepin' in this here bed!"

Bessie went over to the second bed, crawling on her hands and knees. "And if I don't miss my guess, somebody's been a-snorin' away in my bed, too!"

A long pause followed. Mountie O'Teale, a shy ten-year-old, inched her way toward the center of the stage. Her face had been darkened with a piece of coal—Christy's version of stage makeup.

Mountie suffered from a speech impediment, but with Christy's help, she'd made a lot of progress. Christy had hoped that giving Mountie a speaking role would boost the little girl's confidence. Now, seeing her nervous expression, she wasn't so sure.

"Go ahead, Mountie," Christy said gently.

Mountie started to speak. She glanced back at Creed, who gave a nod.

"Some . . . somebody's been . . ." Mountie began.

"Keep going, Mountie," Christy whispered. "You can do it!"

"Some . . . somebody's been a-sleepin' in my bed," Mountie said, "and—and—"

Several students snickered. "Hush," Christy said sternly. "Go on, Mountie. Pull on the sheet and say your line."

Mountie went to the smallest bed and grasped the edge of the sheet. Goldilocks lay hidden, breathing steadily.

"Somebody's been a-sleepin' in my bed," Mountie repeated, "and here she is!"

She yanked on the sheet. For a moment, all was still. Then, suddenly, uproarious laughter filled the room.

Lizette was not on the bed.

In her place was Mabel, one of the resident hogs who lived under the schoolhouse. She snored away, undisturbed by the commotion around her. Lizette emerged from the spot behind the bed where she'd been hiding. "Looks to me like ol' Goldilocks has been eatin' *way* too much of our porridge!" she exclaimed.

Mabel opened one eye. She looked over at Lizette and gave a disgusted snort.

Mountie ran over to Christy, her face alight. "Did we fool you, Teacher?"

"I'll say!" Christy said, shaking her head. "It was a wonderful joke, children."

"When you was in school plays," Ruby Mae asked, "did you have this much fun, Miz Christy?"

Christy smiled. "Those were some of the best days of my life, Ruby Mae. But to tell you the truth, you are the finest cast I've ever had the pleasure to work with." She gave Mountie a hug. "Now, how about if we rehearse the whole play from the beginning? Only this time, let's try it without Mabel in the starring role!"

❧ TWO ❧

That afternoon when the children had left, Christy stood on the empty "stage." They'd truly seemed to enjoy themselves today, and so had she. On days like this, she loved teaching with all her heart. She just knew she was doing the work God had always intended for her to do.

Of course, she hadn't always been so sure she wanted to be a teacher. In fact, in high school back in Asheville, North Carolina, Christy had been certain that she was destined for the New York stage. Well, maybe not *certain*. But she had dreamed about it from time to time, especially after her performance in *Romeo and Juliet*. Everyone said she'd been the best Juliet in the history of Asheville High School.

She could still see the lovely balcony set.

She could still remember her silken gown, the one her mother had lovingly stitched for her. She could still remember every line as if it were yesterday. . . .

"O Romeo, Romeo, wherefore art thou Romeo?" Christy whispered.

Slowly she recited the words she knew so well, her voice swelling with feeling. She clasped her hands before her, eyes closed, as she repeated Shakespeare's famous lines as if they were her own.

Suddenly a familiar voice met her ears. "But, soft, what light through yonder window breaks? It is the east, and Juliet is the sun."

Christy's eyes flew open. Doctor MacNeill was standing in the doorway, arms crossed over his chest. He was a big, handsomely rugged man. His curly hair was unruly, and his hazel eyes were accented by smile lines. He stood there with an amused expression on his face.

"Neil!" Christy cried, her face burning with embarrassment. "How . . . how long have you been standing there?"

The doctor made his way past the maze of desks. "Long enough to tell you've been hiding your true talent from the rest of us. That was quite moving, if I do say so myself. Although I'm no theater critic."

"No Shakespeare buff, either," Christy replied. "You got your line wrong."

"I was overwhelmed by your delivery," the doctor said. His voice was teasing, but she could see the affection in his eyes. Doctor MacNeill had made no secret about his feelings for Christy. Still, he often hid them behind a wall of teasing and humor.

"I take it you're saying I'm no great Romeo?" the doctor inquired as he helped Christy move some of the props.

"Well, let's just say you're an improvement over the Romeo I starred with in high school— Joseph McPratt, Jr. He tended to spit when he delivered his lines. Especially the romantic ones."

The doctor clucked his tongue. "How unfortunate."

"Oh, well. I guess my career as an actress was doomed before it even took off."

"How's the play shaping up?"

Christy draped a sheet over one of the beds. "We had a last-minute cast change today. Mabel stood in for Lizette in the role of Goldilocks. It was quite a performance."

"She can be a bit of a ham, if you know what I mean." The doctor grinned. "You know, all of Cutter Gap's looking forward to the show tomorrow afternoon. I hope my Aunt Cora makes it here in time. She'd get a real kick out of it."

"She's due to get in this evening, isn't she?"

"It depends on the roads. With all the rain we've had lately, it's pretty slow going. It'll be good to see her. It's been almost six years."

"Well, I'm not sure a woman from a town as sophisticated as Knoxville will be all that impressed with our version of the theater."

"Oh, Aunt Cora loves the theater in any form. Did I tell you she directs plays for the Knoxville Players?"

Christy gasped. "Neil! Your aunt directs the Knoxville Players and you forgot to *tell* me? They're the finest acting company in Tennessee!" She squeezed his arm. "And you forgot to *tell* me?"

"It slipped my mind," Doctor MacNeill shrugged. "And let go of my arm, woman. You're cutting off the circulation."

"This is terrible. She's going to see our pathetic little play and laugh and laugh," Christy moaned. "Neil, don't let her come. Promise me you won't let her come. If I know she's in the audience, I'll be petrified."

The doctor laughed. "Christy, you're not acting in the play. A bunch of children are—children who never even heard the word *play* till you introduced it to them. And I think my aunt can tell the difference between the Cutter Gap production of *Goldilocks and the Three Bears* and Shakespeare."

"You're right," Christy admitted. "I don't

11

know what got into me. Sorry. I suppose I always thought maybe I'd star in a real play someday. . . ." She gave an embarrassed smile. "It's crazy, I know."

"Not at all. You forget I just witnessed your brilliant performance as Juliet."

"You're just being sweet."

"No, I'm just being honest." The doctor dropped to one knee. "Let's see if I still remember my college English class . . ." He cleared his throat, grasped Christy's hands in his and began to recite more lines:

> *Good night, good night! Parting is such*
> *   sweet sorrow,*
> *That I shall say good night till it be morrow.*

Just then, David appeared in the doorway. He took one look at the doctor on his knees and loudly cleared his throat. "Excuse me for interrupting." He looked at Doctor MacNeill. "I came to tell you your aunt's just arrived at the mission house." He paused, scratching his head. "What exactly *am* I interrupting, anyway?"

Quickly, Doctor MacNeill got to his feet. "Just some terribly bad acting, I'm afraid, Reverend. I was doing my best to impress Christy with my Shakespeare."

David rolled his eyes. "In my experience, it takes more than that to impress Christy."

"Actually, I wasn't very impressed," Christy said. She winked at David. "The sad truth is, Neil, you were reciting *Juliet's* lines."

❧ Three ❧

So, Neil tells me you're a bit of a theater buff yourself, Christy," the doctor's aunt said that evening at dinner.

"She's the best director in Cutter Gap," exclaimed Ruby Mae, who lived at the mission house with Christy and Miss Ida. "'Course, factually speakin', she's the *only* one."

Cora Gray laughed loudly. "Ruby Mae, my dear, that's the best kind of director to be. Too many cooks spoil the broth, if you get my meaning."

"Truth to tell, I don't rightly follow you—" Ruby Mae began.

"Remember the other day, Ruby Mae," Christy said, "when you tried to convince me we should change the name of our play to *Goldilocks and the Six Bears* so that the understudies could perform, too? That's what Aunt Cora means by 'too many cooks.'"

"I weren't cookin'. I was directin'," Ruby Mae muttered as she reached for the bowl of Miss Ida's mashed potatoes.

Doctor MacNeil's aunt was so down-to-earth and charming that Christy already felt like she'd known her forever. She was a plump, animated woman with vivid blue eyes and a full-throated laugh you could hear in the next county. From the minute she'd arrived, she'd insisted that everyone call her "Aunt Cora."

"Aunt Cora, you'll be interested to hear that Christy once starred in *Romeo and Juliet*," the doctor said.

"So did your nephew," David added wryly. "I caught a bit of his performance this afternoon."

Doctor MacNeill pretended to pout. "Personally, I thought I made a riveting Juliet."

"I was just in a high school play, Aunt Cora," Christy explained quickly. "It was nothing, really."

"Right now, the Knoxville Players is working on a production of *Romeo and Juliet*," said Aunt Cora. "There's nothing tougher than Shakespeare."

"I wish I could see it," Christy said. "It's been so long since I've watched a real play. Not since I was living in Asheville."

"Cutter Gap doesn't get much in the way of the arts," Miss Alice explained with a smile. "That's why we're all so excited about Christy's play."

"Theater is my great love," Aunt Cora said. "When those curtains part and the lights dim, it's simply magical."

Christy couldn't help sighing. "That's how it always felt to me, too," she said. "I actually used to dream . . ." She hesitated, suddenly self-conscious.

"Dream what, dear?" Aunt Cora asked gently.

Christy shrugged. "Oh, you know—silly things. I dreamed that I'd someday be in a real play on a real stage."

"That was my very dream when I was growing up!" Aunt Cora said with a smile. "Don't forget: 'We are such stuff as dreams are made on.'" She winked at Ruby Mae. "That's from another one of Shakespeare's plays."

"He sure did write a heap," Ruby Mae said.

"I suppose he was a bit of a dreamer himself." Aunt Cora took a sip of her tea. "I like to think we all are."

"Oh, I got powerful plenty o' dreams," said Ruby Mae. "I want to be a mama in a big house in a fancy city, like Asheville—maybe even Knoxville. And I'll have me a golden horse, faster 'n lightnin'."

Aunt Cora nodded. "Those are fine dreams, Ruby Mae," she said.

"How about the rest o' you?" Ruby Mae asked. "Miss Alice, I'll bet you got yourself all kinds o' fine dreams."

Miss Alice considered. "That's a good question. I have lots of dreams, I suppose. To begin with, I dream of bringing medicine and learning and hope to every last person in these mountains." She grinned. "And of course, there's my long-held aspiration to learn to play the dulcimer."

"Why, Miss Alice, I'm sure Jeb Spencer would learn you to play, if'n you just asked him," Ruby Mae exclaimed.

"It's true, Miss Alice," Christy added. "Jeb's taught all of his children how to play. And it's such a lovely instrument."

Christy could still remember the first time she'd heard Jeb play the dulcimer. It was a box-like instrument with four strings, a slender waist and heart-shaped holes. The sweet music it made sounded as if it had been sent straight from heaven.

"How about you, Preacher?" Ruby Mae asked. "What's your dream?"

David combed back his straight, dark hair with his fingers. He thought for a moment before answering. "Well, to tell you the truth, Ruby Mae," he said, "I wouldn't mind seeing more of the world someday. Paris. London.

The mysterious Far East." He shrugged. "Of course, it'll probably never happen. It's hard to imagine having the time, let alone the money. . . ."

"You can't go a-thinkin' that way, Preacher," Ruby Mae scolded. She reached across the table to snare the last of Miss Ida's flaky biscuits. "You gotta keep hopin'. That's the fun o' dreamin'."

"Ruby Mae's right," Miss Alice agreed. "When I told people I was going to help start a mission here in the Great Smokies, you should have heard their reactions. They said I was doomed to fail." She grinned. "Some even said I was crazy. But you have to dream big, even if you might fail. The trying is everything."

Miss Ida cleared her throat. "Well, I should see to the cleaning up, I suppose." She pushed back her chair and began to clear the table.

"Hold on, Miss Ida," Christy said. "You can't get away without telling us your dream."

"I don't have a dream," Miss Ida said primly. "Unless, of course, it's that someday Ruby Mae will finally learn to clean up her bedroom."

"Not so fast, Ida." David yanked on her apron string. "I admitted my dream. Fair is fair."

"I'm telling you, I don't have a dream," Miss Ida insisted. She pulled free of David's grasp and marched toward the kitchen. When she got to the door, she paused.

"Unless," she said, turning to look at the group with a little smile, "you count my secret dream to become a tap dancer." She demonstrated with a couple of quick steps, and vanished into the kitchen.

"Well, well," said Doctor MacNeill. "That's a side of Miss Ida we've never seen before!" He consulted his pocket watch. "I should be heading back to my cabin, folks. I want to make a stop on the way home and check on the Millers' new baby."

"Not so fast, Neil." Christy wagged her finger at him. "You're the only one who hasn't revealed a dream. We're not letting you escape that easily."

The doctor shrugged. "These days, I generally avoid dreaming. Real life is complicated enough. Seems to me having dreams just sets you up for failure."

"This, from a man who decided to practice medicine in such a remote corner of the world?" said Aunt Cora. "I'd call that quite a big dream."

"Come on," Ruby Mae urged, "just tell us one itty-bitty teensy-weensy dream. Ain't there somethin' you always wanted to learn yourself how to do? Like whittlin'?"

"Or playing the trombone?" Christy suggested.

"Or attending church regularly?" David added with a sly grin.

"Nope." Doctor MacNeill folded his arms over his chest. "Not a one."

"You're not leaving this table until you admit something," Christy warned.

The doctor rubbed his chin. "I can see I'm vastly outnumbered. All right. Maybe there is *one* thing. But you have to promise not to laugh. Especially you, Reverend."

"You have my solemn vow," David responded.

"I've always wanted to . . . well, learn how to paint. The mountains are so beautiful, I sometimes wish I could capture them on canvas forever." The doctor shook his head. "There. Now that I've made a complete fool of myself, are you all happy?"

"Neil, that's not the least bit foolish," Christy said gently. "I think it's a wonderful dream."

"And so do I," pronounced Aunt Cora. "Perhaps I'll send you some painting supplies when I get back to Knoxville."

"Oh, I wouldn't have the time," Doctor MacNeil said. "Don't bother, Aunt—"

"No bother. Who knows? We may have a budding artistic genius in our midst." She nudged Christy. "Not to mention a budding theatrical genius. Your play tomorrow could be the start of something wonderful."

"Well, it's a little smaller scale than the Knoxville Players. But it's the finest company of actors in the world."

❧ Four ❧

And now, I'd like everyone in our little theater company to take a final bow!"

It was the following afternoon. The play had been a wonderful success. Christy watched in delight as all of her students gathered at the front of the schoolroom. Everyone was there—the stagehands, the set decorators, the understudies, and the actors—even Little Burl, the curtain-puller.

The rest of the room was filled to capacity. Parents, grandparents, great-grandparents, younger sisters and brothers—it seemed as if everyone in Cutter Gap had shown up for the debut performance of *Goldilocks*. So many people had come, in fact, that many of them had been forced to watch the show through the windows.

Now they stood on their feet, applauding

and stomping and cheering and whistling. Christy held up her hand, and at her signal, all seventy students bowed, just the way she'd taught them. Slowly, Little Burl tugged the curtain across the stage.

"I want to thank you all for coming to our first performance," Christy called, but the audience was still applauding wildly and she could barely make herself heard.

She slipped behind the curtain. "Wonderful job, everybody!" she said to the excited students. She could see the pride shining in their eyes.

"They's still a-clappin' and carryin' on, Teacher," Creed exclaimed. "Ain't it a wonder?"

"They're clapping so hard because you deserve it," Christy said. "You know, I think that after all this excitement, I'm going to go ahead and dismiss class for the day. You all can head on out and find your families. Congratulations, everyone, on a wonderful performance!"

A few minutes later, David, Aunt Cora, and Doctor MacNeill made their way through the crowd to congratulate Christy.

"What a turnout!" David exclaimed. "And they were hanging on every word. I wish I could get these people to pay as close attention to my sermons!"

"Maybe if you dressed up in a bear costume, Reverend," Doctor MacNeill joked.

"You did a wonderful job, Christy," Aunt Cora said. "Those children just lit up the stage."

"I'm so proud of them," Christy said. "Especially children like Mountie O'Teale, the one who played Baby Bear. She's always been very shy around people. For a long time she even refused to speak. But there she was, out on that little stage, saying her lines like an old acting pro!"

"Christy," Aunt Cora said, "there's something I'd like to discuss with you." She exchanged a glance with Doctor MacNeill. "Please feel free to say no if you're not interested. I mean, I know how busy you are here with the school, and the timing isn't the best . . ."

"What is it?" Christy asked.

"Well, as I told you, our production of *Romeo and Juliet* begins soon. Because I'd planned this trip for so long, I left the play in the capable hands of my assistant director. Still, when I get back to Knoxville, there'll be plenty of last-minute chaos to contend with. I was wondering if you'd like to come back with me and help out with the production. I might even be able to get you a small part in the play."

Christy just stared in disbelief. She couldn't be quite sure, but she had the feeling that her mouth was hanging open.

"Christy," Doctor MacNeill elbowed her, "you're in distinct danger of drooling."

"I . . . I don't know what to say," Christy managed. "I mean, I'm so flattered that you asked, Aunt Cora. And it would be such an honor to help you. But I have my obligations here. The children, my work . . . I just couldn't . . ."

"Ah, but we're way ahead of you," said Doctor MacNeill. "The Reverend and Miss Alice have already agreed to take over your teaching duties while you're gone."

"Go on, Christy," David urged. "It'd do you good. Miss Alice and I can handle things just fine."

"I might even go along with you," said Doctor MacNeill. "I've got some friends in Knoxville—doctors I went to school with. And I'd love to spend more time with Aunt Cora."

"But I couldn't begin to afford a ticket—"

"It's my treat," Aunt Cora interrupted. "You'd be doing me a favor, actually. I'd welcome your help. It's the first rule of the theater: the last few days before a play debuts, things always seem to go wrong."

Christy hesitated. "But my going would be so silly, really. I'm not an actress. I'm not a director. I'm a teacher."

"It's a once-in-a-lifetime chance, Christy," said Doctor MacNeill. "You can't pass it up. It's your dream."

"I—I'll think about it," Christy stuttered. "Would that be all right, Aunt Cora?"

"Of course." Aunt Cora patted Christy on the shoulder. "You take all the time you need. But remember this line from Shakespeare, dear:

Our doubts are traitors,
And make us lose the good we oft might win,
By fearing to attempt.

Doctor MacNeill grinned. "Translation— what have you got to lose?"

"Nothing, I suppose . . ." Christy said. Under her breath she added, "except my pride."

❧ Five ❧

I just don't know what to do, Miss Alice."

A week had passed, and Christy still hadn't made up her mind about Aunt Cora's offer. This afternoon, after school had let out, Christy had come to Miss Alice's cabin, hoping to get some much-needed advice.

"I have to decide something soon," Christy said. "Aunt Cora's going back to Knoxville in two days."

Miss Alice, dressed in a crisp dark green linen skirt and white blouse, was brewing tea. She turned to Christy, smiling. "Try looking at things this way. What's the worse thing that could happen if you went on this little adventure?"

Christy sank into a rocking chair. "The worst thing? Well, I'd be abandoning my students. They might lose ground on their spelling and grammar work. And I'm just starting to get some discipline in my classroom. That could all go down the drain."

"In a few days' time? Don't you think David and I are competent to handle things?"

"Of course," Christy said quickly. "I suppose I'm just feeling guilty about leaving my students. Even if it is for just a little while."

Miss Alice poured steaming tea into two china teacups painted with dainty pink roses. She handed one to Christy, then sat beside her. "Well, what else could go wrong? Let's look a little deeper."

"Well, I could just get in Aunt Cora's way, for one thing. I doubt she really needs my help. She's just being kind."

"What makes you say that?"

"I don't know the first thing about the theater, not really. Not like she does."

"I'm sure you could help out in any number of ways," Miss Alice argued. "And besides, you have had some experience in the theater."

"That was in high school, Miss Alice—not professional theater!" Christy sipped the hot peppermint tea. "Or were you referring to my directing debut at the Cutter Gap Community Theater?"

Miss Alice laughed. "Everyone has to start somewhere."

"Suppose I did go to Knoxville," Christy said, "and I actually managed to land a role on stage. I'm sure I'd end up tripping on my skirt or forgetting my lines. Just imagine how embarrassing *that* would be!"

"So the worst thing you can imagine is that you might trip on stage, in front of hundreds of people?"

"Well, it *would* be pretty humiliating, don't you think?" Christy cried.

"Being embarrassed is part of being human, Christy. We all make mistakes. We all try things and fail. The important thing is that we do try—and keep trying. That's what God wants from us. That we try. That we do our best. He doesn't expect perfection."

"I know. But still . . ." Christy's voice trailed off.

"Do you recall when you first came here to teach?" Miss Alice asked. "Remember how discouraged you were, faced with such a huge class? I told you a story about a baby."

Christy nodded. "It was about a baby learning to walk. How he wobbles and falls and maybe even bumps his nose. But he just gets up and tries again. He doesn't care what anybody thinks. All he cares about is learning to walk. Oh yes, I remember." She gave a laugh. "You're saying if I fall on my fanny in front of hundreds of people, I should just brush myself off like that baby and try again?"

"That's exactly what I'm saying. As I told

you before, we Quakers like to say that all discouragement is from an evil source, and that it can only end in more evil. The important thing is that you will have tried something new and difficult. And you will have learned and grown as a person. That's all that matters."

Christy gazed out the bank of windows across the back of the room. It was a breathtaking view. The towering peaks and lush greenery spread out before them like a gigantic painting. No wonder the doctor wished he could capture a scene like this on canvas.

She wondered if he would ever try his hand at painting. Probably not. He was too proud, too afraid to fail at something he thought was "silly."

Christy pursed her lips. "Are you absolutely sure that you and David can handle things?"

"Absolutely and positively."

"All right, then." Christy set down her teacup and leapt to her feet. "I'm going to give it a try. I may look foolish. But I'm going to do it!"

"Wonderful!"

Christy's hand flew to her mouth. "I haven't even started packing! And I've got to put lesson plans together, and tell Aunt Cora, and . . . oh, dear, Miss Alice! I've got to go!"

"Can't you even finish your tea?"

"I don't think so. I'm too excited."

Miss Alice watched, grinning, as Christy raced for the door. "Christy?" she called.

"Yes?"

"I was going to say 'break a leg.' After all, it's an expression of good luck in the theater. But I'm afraid you're so frantic, you might just take me literally."

"How about giving me a hug instead?" Christy asked, rushing to her side.

"Even better," Miss Alice agreed.

≈ Six ≈

I can't believe I'm really on this train," Christy whispered. "I'm not dreaming this, am I?"

Doctor MacNeill pinched his arm. "No. I seem to be quite awake. I definitely felt that. How about you, Aunt Cora?"

Aunt Cora was seated across from the doctor and Christy on the red velvet seat. "I'm happy to report I'm quite awake," she said.

They had spent the previous afternoon traveling from Cutter Gap to the small town of El Pano. There, they'd spent the night at a boardinghouse. Christy had stayed there on her first trip to Cutter Gap months earlier. Now, at last, they were on their way to Knoxville.

"My, my," Aunt Cora said, her head cocked to one side.

"What?" the doctor asked.

"Has anyone ever told you two you make a rather handsome couple?"

Christy felt certain she'd turned as red as the cushions. But Doctor MacNeill just winked. "I think what you have here is more like the pairing of Beauty and the Beast, Aunt Cora."

"Neil's just being modest," Christy whispered to Aunt Cora.

Christy lay back against the cushion and watched the deep green forests flash past. Riding in this train reminded her of her trip to Tennessee several months ago to begin her work in Cutter Gap.

The smells and sights and sounds were so familiar! The scent of coal dust in the railroad car. The brass spittoons. The potbellied stove in the rear. The sacks of grain and produce piled toward the back. And, of course, the shrill whistle of the train.

The car rocked gently back and forth. The steady click-click-click of the wheels was deeply soothing. Christy's eyelids were heavy, but she didn't want to sleep. She couldn't let herself miss a moment of this adventure.

In the window glass, she caught sight of her reflection. Again she was reminded of that cold day last January. That's when she'd left her parents' home in Asheville to teach school at the Cutter Gap Mission in the Smoky Mountains. She was wearing the same fawn-colored coatsuit, but she had changed in many other ways. Her hair was longer now and streaked by the sun. Her skin was bronzed. Her hands were calloused from working in Miss Ida's garden. She looked older than her nineteen years, and maybe even a little bit wiser.

She'd been so afraid that January day! And she'd felt so very alone. Now, here she was, seated next to two good friends, with so many more back home in Cutter Gap. Perhaps that was the most important—and the most wonderful—change of all.

Christy reached into her satchel and pulled out her diary. "Are you taking notes?" Aunt Cora inquired.

"This is my diary. I started it when I left Asheville to teach in Cutter Gap."

Christy opened to the first page. There, in her pretty, flowing handwriting, was the entry she'd made her first day:

The truth is, I have not been this afraid before, or felt this alone and homesick. Leaving everyone I love was harder than I thought it would be. But I must be strong. I am at the start of a great adventure. And great adventures are sometimes scary.

Doctor MacNeill peeked over Christy's arm.

"I'll bet that's interesting reading. Do I make an appearance?"

Christy slapped the little book shut. "You're as bad as George." She winked at Aunt Cora. "That's my younger brother. I used to keep my old diary under lock and key to prevent him from sneaking a peek at it. Once he actually managed to open it with a screwdriver. Fortunately, I caught him just in the nick of time." She pointed her finger at the doctor. "Trespassers will be prosecuted to the full extent of the law, Neil."

He held up his hands in a gesture of surrender. "Fine, fine. I guess I'll just have to take a nap instead."

He leaned back against the seat and closed his eyes. Aunt Cora opened up her book of Shakespeare's plays and began to read. Confident she could write in privacy, Christy got out her pen and began to write. The jiggling railroad car made it difficult to be neat, but she did the best she could:

> *I'm on another adventure! And I'm almost as nervous as I was the day I headed to Cutter Gap on that train, pulled by the engine everyone called "Old Buncombe."*
>
> *Of course, this time I know there's not so much at stake. As Miss Alice pointed out, I have nothing to lose but some dignity. And who knows what I might learn from this experience?*

As we were leaving Cutter Gap, Miss Alice whispered something in my ear, a favorite Bible quote of hers: "He which soweth bountifully shall reap also bountifully."

I think what she was trying to tell me was that there is no telling what I might gain from taking this risk.

But fear is a funny thing. I feel excited and nervous all the way down to my toes. My stomach's doing flip-flops. I'm still hours away from Knoxville, and nowhere near that big theater where I may actually make my big-city debut.

I know the worst that can happen—I'll end up a little humbler. That wouldn't be such a bad thing, would it? Still and all, it would be awfully nice if I could shake this feeling that I'm getting in way over my head.

Christy closed up her diary and tucked it into her satchel. Telephone poles flew past outside her window.

Doctor MacNeill opened one eye. "Done writing?"

"For now, anyway."

He smiled. "I sure would like to know what's in that diary of yours. It's tantalizing, knowing that the secrets of your heart are only a few inches away."

"If you want to read a diary, you'll have to get one of your own, Neil."

"Now, *that* would be some boring reading,"

he replied. "Try to get some sleep. It's a long trip."

"How can you sleep? I'm too excited—and nervous."

"Nervous?" Doctor MacNeill asked. "What's there to be nervous about?"

Christy grinned. "Nothing, I hope. But I guess I'll find out soon enough."

⊱ Seven ⊰

Look out, Aunt Cora!" Christy cried, for what had to be the dozenth time.

Aunt Cora braked her car in the nick of time, narrowly avoiding a man pulling a mule and a small cart. "Whoopsie," she said with a smile.

It was early evening when they arrived at the train station in Knoxville. Aunt Cora had insisted on driving home. She'd left her old car parked in the street, right in front of the station. Doctor MacNeill had offered to drive, but Aunt Cora wouldn't hear of it.

"Nonsense. You haven't driven since you were in medical school, and then it was just when your friend Peter Mulberry would lend you his old rattletrap," Aunt Cora had said firmly. "And it's not like you have the opportunity to drive much in Cutter Gap, Neil.

Trust me. Ever since your Uncle Robert died, I've taken care of all the driving. And I'm a natural, if I do say so myself."

Now, after several minutes of lurching stops and breathtaking turns, Christy wasn't so sure. Aunt Cora was so busy pointing out the sights that she often lost track of the road.

"And over there—see that little white clapboard church? That's where Neil's Uncle Robert and I were married."

"It's lovely, Aunt Cora," Christy replied, gripping the seat till her knuckles were white. "By the way, I think you were supposed to stop back there—"

"Pish. I checked. Didn't see a thing." Aunt Cora pointed out the window with her gloved hand. "And that park over there? That's where Neil and his cousin Lucy used to play when they came to visit us in the summer. Remember, Neil? You were cute as a button—"

"Aunt Cora?" The doctor cleared his throat. "I think that fruit truck was honking at us."

"People can be so rude!" she muttered.

Finally, to Christy's great relief, Aunt Cora stopped the car in the driveway of a lovely, white brick home.

Sitting in a rocker on the porch was a thin, balding man with wire-rimmed spectacles. He was bent over, elbows on his knees, hands cupping his chin. He looked very forlorn.

"Oh my," Aunt Cora whispered. "It's Oliver. This doesn't look good at all—not at all."

"Who's Oliver?" asked Doctor MacNeill.

Aunt Cora waved at the man, who simply gave a sullen nod.

"Oliver Flump," she explained, "is the assistant director of the Knoxville Players. He's a very nice man, but he tends to get a little . . . well, *flustered* sometimes. The slightest little thing will set him into a tizzy. I left him in charge of the play in the hope it would boost his self-confidence."

"He doesn't look very self-confident," Christy said.

"No, indeed he doesn't. Well—" Aunt Cora flung open the car door, "I suppose we might as well see what the problem is. I'm sure it's nothing. It usually is."

While the doctor retrieved their bags, Christy and Aunt Cora joined Oliver on the porch.

"Mr. Oliver Flump, I'd like you to meet Miss Christy Huddleston of Cutter Gap, Tennessee."

"How do you do, Miss Huddleston?" Oliver said. He had a mournful, high voice. It reminded Christy of one of Jeb Spencer's hound dogs, whining for supper.

"It's nice to meet you, Mr. Flump."

"Please, call me Oliver. Everybody does."

"Are you just here as a one-man welcoming committee, Oliver?" Aunt Cora asked. She held open the front door. Christy headed inside, followed by a slouching Oliver. "Or has something gone wrong with the play?"

Oliver went straight to the parlor and dropped into an overstuffed chair. He groaned. "It's too awful to say out loud. My career in the theater is doomed. That's all I have to say on the subject. One word—*doomed*."

"That's what you said when we did our last play. And the play before that, as I recall," said Aunt Cora. "Christy, come. Help me light the lamps while Oliver recounts his tale of woe."

"This time it's no laughing matter, Cora," Oliver said defensively.

"What have I told you about that hangdog attitude, Oliver?" Aunt Cora asked cheerfully as she lit a lamp near the mantel. "How will anyone else ever believe in Oliver Flump, if he doesn't believe in himself?"

Christy lit a lamp on a walnut table next to Oliver. "You have a lovely home, Aunt Cora."

"Why, thank you, Christy. See the framed theater programs on the wall? Those are from my days in New York City. I was much younger then—thinner, too—" she added with a chuckle. "I must have seen every show I could afford, and more I couldn't. Sometimes I just got the inexpensive seats up in the balcony. Oh, but the plays I saw performed! All of Shakespeare's comedies, and most of his tragedies! Oh, my—" she put her hand to her heart, "what days those were!"

Doctor MacNeill entered, carrying the bags. "Shall I put these upstairs?"

"No, no. Come sit a spell. We'll make a fire in the fireplace, and Oliver will tell us his tale of woe. Oliver, meet my nephew, Doctor Neil MacNeill. Finest physician in the entire United States. I'd say the whole world, but I don't want to sound like a boastful relative."

The doctor shook Oliver's hand. "I understand you're Aunt Cora's right-hand man."

"No longer. Not after all that's happened." Oliver sighed. "I'm doomed, you see—and so is our play."

Aunt Cora clucked her tongue. "Oliver, dear. Please tell me what's wrong, without any dramatics." She sat down on the couch across from him. "I'm sure we can make a quick fix of it. You know you have a tendency to over-react."

"I most certainly do not!" Oliver cried.

"Remember the posters for *The Taming of the Shrew*? Remember how you offered to resign over them? Three times, as I recall."

"That was a definite crisis," Oliver explained to Christy and the doctor. "You see, they'd printed them wrong. The posters read '*The*

Taming of the Shoe.' Who, I ask you, wants to see a play about a shoe?"

"At least it was a tame shoe," Aunt Cora said lightly, "and not one of those wild, ferocious, man-eating shoes."

"It wasn't funny, Cora." Oliver rubbed his eyes. "It was a nightmare—a true nightmare."

"Nonsense," Aunt Cora said. "We all got a good laugh out of it."

"Well, try getting a laugh out of this," Oliver said bitterly. "Sarah McGeorge has laryngitis. She can't even whisper her lines."

"No problem. Pansy Trotman will make a fine Juliet," Aunt Cora said with a wave of her hand. "She's Sarah's understudy," she explained.

Oliver folded his arms over his chest. "And as if that weren't enough, the entire theater company is threatening to quit unless *I* quit!"

"Oh, my," said Aunt Cora. "That is a bit of a pickle, I must admit. Have you been short with them, Oliver? You know you can be rather demanding."

"I have most certainly not been short with them," Oliver replied. "In fact, I've exhibited saintly patience, despite their insults and belligerence."

"Well, I'll have a little talk with them. We'll work things out."

"It's too late." Oliver sighed. "I'm resigning.

The production is yours. The truth is, I'm glad to be done with it. This play is doomed."

≈ Eight ≈

There it is," Aunt Cora said the next morning, "my home away from home. Isn't it beautiful?"

Christy gazed at the ornate brass doors of the theater. A large poster at the ticket window announced the upcoming production of *Romeo and Juliet*. In the bright sun, the whole building seemed to shimmer.

"I can't believe we're really here," she whispered.

"We're here, all right." Aunt Cora swung open the doors. "Come on. I'll introduce you and Neil to all the gang."

Christy and the doctor followed Aunt Cora through the silent, empty lobby. An oriental carpet covered the floor. Posters from other performances hung on the walls.

Aunt Cora led them to another set of doors. "Hear that yelling in there?" she asked. "Welcome to the glamorous world of the theater!"

Doctor MacNeill opened the doors. Christy gasped. There, spread before her, was the theater of her dreams—the hundreds of seats, the broad stage, the thick velvet curtains. Everything was just as she'd imagined it.

On the stage, a large group of people hurried to and fro. Some were carrying pages, reciting lines to themselves. Some had paint cans or brushes. A young boy was hammering away at a wooden set.

In the center of all the turmoil was a familiar face. "Isn't that Oliver?" Christy asked.

"I knew he wouldn't really resign," said Aunt Cora. "He never does. He loves the theater as much as I do."

"I am *not* overacting," a young man cried from the stage. "I am emoting! I am having emotions, Oliver! You, on the other hand, are not directing! You are *dictating*!"

Aunt Cora hustled down the aisle, clapping her hands to get attention. Christy smiled. It reminded her of her own attempt at directing seventy schoolchildren.

"People, please!" Aunt Cora yelled. "Let's have a little civility! We have guests!" She crooked a finger. "Christy, Neil, come sit down here. You can have front-row seats today. Tomorrow I'll really put you to work, Christy."

"Cora's back!" somebody yelled, and the people on stage broke into applause.

"Thank goodness!" someone else said. "The reign of terror is over!"

Oliver threw up his hands. "See, Cora? Do you see what I've had to put up with in your absence?"

"You!" cried a dark-haired woman in a purple silk dress. She raced to the edge of the stage. "Cora, Oliver has been a tyrant! An absolute tyrant! He's been changing my set designs, belittling the actors, and nit-picking over every little detail! He's been impossible. What a relief it is to have you back!"

"Now, now. Let's everyone settle down." Aunt Cora took a seat next to Christy. "As I told you all before, Oliver is in charge of this production. I am here to offer advice and hold hands and dry tears. But in the end, Oliver is the boss."

"Then I quit!" the woman shouted.

"Me too!" someone else cried.

"You can't quit," Oliver said, "because I'm quitting first!"

"You already quit," said the dark-haired woman. "But here you are, back again, like a bad penny."

A young man with curly brown hair and the wide, innocent eyes of a fawn stepped forward. "It's like this, Cora," he said calmly. "We just can't work with Oliver, not when he's in charge." He cast an apologetic glance at Oliver. "He just plain gets too upset. And when he gets upset, I get upset. And when I get upset, well . . . I can't remember my lines, no matter how hard I try." He shoved his hands in his pockets and shrugged. "I guess what I'm saying is, if Oliver stays, I have to go. That means you will have lost your Romeo *and* your Juliet. Although, of course, the understudies could handle things just fine." He shrugged again. "Anyway, that's my two-cents' worth."

Aunt Cora hesitated. "Oliver, what should we do about this situation? The cast seems to think you've been rather demanding."

"They're prima donnas, all of them," Oliver sniffed. "They don't realize that pain is the price of perfection."

"One thing I've learned from this job, Oliver," said Aunt Cora, "perfectionism can get in the way of having a good time. Suppose you and I direct this production together? Share the power, as it were? Maybe next time you can take a whack at running the show yourself."

Oliver's shoulders slumped. "It's no use. I tried to give it another shot, but clearly, if I'm not wanted . . ."

"Of course you're wanted," Aunt Cora soothed.

"No, he isn't," snapped the dark-haired woman.

"Fine. Then I quit—for real this time," Oliver cried. With that, he stomped off stage and disappeared.

"Arabella," Aunt Cora said, "you didn't have to be so cruel."

"I wasn't being cruel—just truthful," Arabella said. "Oliver's fine as an assistant director, Cora. But whenever you put him in charge, he goes mad with the power."

Aunt Cora climbed the steps to the stage. "Well, I guess the important thing to do right now is get down to business. First of all, I want to introduce you to Miss Christy Huddleston and Doctor Neil MacNeill. Both are from Cutter Gap, Tennessee. Some of you may already have met Neil, my nephew. Miss Huddleston is a budding actress and director in her own right, in addition to being a fine teacher. She's here to help out with the production, and perhaps take a walk-on role."

Arabella cleared her throat loudly. "Speaking of roles, Cora. Now that Sarah's lost her voice, I really think I'm perfect to step into the role of Juliet."

"Arabella, we've been through this already. You're the set and costume designer. Not an actress. Besides, we have a wonderful Juliet at the ready, in the person of Pansy Trotman, her understudy."

"But I'd be perfect for the role," Arabella argued. "Just watch."

Arabella put her hand to her heart, sighed, and crumpled to the ground in a heap.

"Arabella, I've seen your crumple before. You are an excellent crumpler. But the part belongs to Pansy." Aunt Cora turned to Christy and the doctor. "The excellent crumpling you've just witnessed was performed by none other than our own Miss Arabella Devaine. She's been designing costumes and sets for us for years."

Arabella got to her feet, clearly pouting.

"That handsome young man over there is Mr. Gilroy Gannon, our fine Romeo," Aunt Cora continued.

Gilroy, the curly-haired man who'd spoken earlier, waved to Christy and Doctor MacNeill.

"Over there is Miss Pansy Trotman, our new Juliet. And painting away on the balcony set back in the corner are Miss Marylou Marsh and her brother Vernon."

The pretty girl with the paintbrush gave a nod. She was thin, with long blond hair and a shy smile.

"Marylou?" Doctor MacNeill asked. "Is that really you?"

Marylou took a few steps forward. Her smile broadened. "Hi, Neil. You look different too. As I recall, you were rather scrawny."

"I met Marylou one summer when I came here to visit Aunt Cora," the doctor explained to Christy.

"Well, I should get back to my painting," Marylou said softly.

"We'll have to get together and talk over old times," the doctor said.

"That's an excellent suggestion!" exclaimed Aunt Cora. "Listen up, everyone! I've just decided to have a party at my home tomorrow evening. We'll call it an early cast party. That way my nephew and Miss Huddleston can get to know everyone. You're all invited, and I expect you all to come!"

"Already she's giving orders," Gilroy said with a smile. "You're as bad as Oliver, Cora."

"No one's as bad as Oliver," Arabella muttered.

"Enough of this," Aunt Cora said. "We're here to rehearse, not complain. Let us begin, as they say, at the beginning. Act one, scene one! Places, everyone!"

⫸ Nine ⫷

"So, Christy," Aunt Cora said at the party the following evening, "what do you think of theater life so far? You've been with us for two days now."

"I think," Christy replied, "it's a lot more like a schoolroom full of unruly children than I'd ever imagined."

Aunt Cora laughed. "Dear, you've hit the nail right on the head!"

The party had been a wonderful success. Aunt Cora's home was filled to overflowing with the cast and crew. After dinner, some of the stagehands had moved Aunt Cora's furniture into the corners so that people could dance. Three musicians had brought their instruments along, and now they were playing a lilting waltz.

Christy already felt as if she knew most of

the cast. Gilroy was the shy, clumsy, loveable Romeo. Pansy was the sweet understudy who was now playing the role of Juliet, so emotional she could instantly cry on cue. Arabella was the sharp-tongued designer. Oliver was the assistant director with a flair for the dramatic.

"I'm surprised Oliver came tonight," Christy whispered to Aunt Cora. They were standing near the fireplace, watching the others come and go.

"I'm not. Oliver loves us all, and we love him, in spite of all the complaining. He's still nursing a grudge, though. You'll notice how he's hovering in a corner, looking forlorn and resentful."

"I haven't seen Pansy tonight," Christy said.

"Nor have I," said Aunt Cora. "She seemed rather distracted today. Perhaps it's the strain of taking on the lead role."

Christy nodded. "That would be enough to make anyone distracted!"

"My, isn't that Marylou that Neil's dancing with?" Aunt Cora asked. "He's quite light on his feet, isn't he?"

"Were they . . . good friends?" Christy asked, trying very hard not to sound jealous.

"Very good," Aunt Cora replied.

As the waltz came to an end, Christy couldn't help wondering just what *very good* meant. Was it possible that Neil and Marylou had been sweethearts once upon a time?

She watched as the doctor bowed politely to Marylou. He paused at the refreshment table, then strode over, munching on a cookie. "You ladies look lovely this evening."

"And you looked lovely on the dance floor," Christy said, a bit frostily.

"You're too kind, Christy. After all, you've had the painful experience of dancing with me."

"What did you do today, while we were at the theater?" Aunt Cora asked. "I do hope you haven't been too bored, dear."

"Nope. Looked up ol' James Briley. He's that old friend of mine from medical school, Christy. The one who invited me to come to Knoxville to work a while back?"

"I take it you said no?" Aunt Cora asked.

"I was sorely tempted," Doctor MacNeill admitted. "But in the end, Christy helped me see that I belonged in Cutter Gap."

"My loss," Aunt Cora said with a sigh. "But Cutter Gap's gain. In any case, you're always welcome to join us at the theater. Or perhaps we could get you started on those art lessons you've always wanted. I've got a neighbor who's a wonderful artist. I'm sure she'd be delighted to teach you the basics while you're here."

Doctor MacNeill laughed. "I'll find something less challenging to do with my time, Aunt Cora!"

The musicians began a new waltz. "Would either of you ladies care to dance?" Doctor MacNeill asked.

For a moment Christy hesitated. "I'd be honored," she replied at last.

It was difficult dancing in such crowded quarters, but somehow everyone managed. Christy and the doctor swept around the room in tight circles, spinning to the lilting music.

"Having fun so far?" the doctor asked.

"Oh, yes."

"Glad you decided to come?"

"Absolutely," Christy replied.

"By the way, I have a feeling Romeo has a long-distance crush on you," the doctor said. "I've noticed him watching you from afar."

"Gilroy?" Christy cried. "He's hardly said two words to me. But speaking of crushes, I noticed Marylou is over by the piano, sneaking rather dreamy-eyed peeks at you. Maybe you should ask her for another dance, Neil." She gave him a rather shy look. "After all, you said you two were old friends."

"I'm not sure 'friends' is quite the right word," the doctor said with a wry grin. "Marylou used to beat me up on a regular basis."

"Marylou? That sweet, tiny thing? Used to beat *you* up?"

The doctor nodded. "Pummeled me into the ground on a regular basis."

Christy couldn't help laughing. "But why?"

"I couldn't tell you. You know how children are. But it was very humiliating. I couldn't fight back, because, of course, my mother had taught me never to hit a girl."

"Come to think of it, I did hear Marylou ask if you ever learned to fight back. It sounds to me like you could have been too scrawny and weak to fight back. Are you sure you *could* have fought back?"

The doctor rolled his eyes. "It's a good thing this waltz is coming to an end. I can see where this conversation is going. You're never going to let me live this down, are you?"

Just as Christy started to respond, Arabella came rushing into the room.

"I have terrible news!" Arabella cried. "The most dreadful, terrible news!"

Everyone fell silent. Arabella ran to Aunt Cora's side. "Come, Cora. I think you should be sitting down when you hear this."

Aunt Cora shook her off impatiently. "Goodness, Arabella! Will you just tell me what's happened? Has someone died?"

"She might as well have." Arabella fanned her face with her hand, as if she were in danger of fainting. "It's Pansy."

"Pansy? What's happened to Pansy?" Aunt Cora demanded.

Arabella paused, glancing around the room to be sure she had everyone's attention. "When dear little Pansy didn't show up for the party, I felt compelled to call her at home to be sure she was well. After all, you know how Pansy loves a party."

"The point, Arabella," Aunt Cora grumbled. "Get to the point."

"Well, her mother answered, and she was positively beside herself, poor woman. Of course, who could blame her? I mean, if Pansy were *my* daughter. . . . Not, mind you, that I'm old enough to have a daughter Pansy's age, but still—"

"The point, Arabella!" Aunt Cora cried.

Arabella took a long, dramatic pause. "Pansy," she said softly, "has eloped!"

"Eloped!" Aunt Cora cried. "With whom?"

"The butcher on Pine Street. You know the one. Mustache, big ears? A nice enough man, but still . . ."

"I *told* you this play was doomed!" Oliver declared triumphantly. "And now you have the proof. Juliet number one loses her voice. And now Juliet number two runs off with a butcher, without so much as a proper farewell! If that's not doomed, I don't know what is! We are officially Juliet-less!"

"Settle down, Oliver. I'm sure we'll think

of something," Aunt Cora said. Still, for the first time since Christy had met her, Aunt Cora looked genuinely worried.

"Speaking as Romeo, this is very hard to take," Gilroy said. "I can't keep falling madly in love with a new Juliet every other day." He sighed. "It's much too confusing."

"How are we ever going to find another Juliet on such short notice?" Aunt Cora asked.

"Look no further, Cora," said Arabella. "*I* shall rescue us from the jaws of defeat. It will be a terrible sacrifice, to be sure—long hours, terrific pressure, even the jealousy of my peers. But through it all, one guiding philosophy will sustain me." She clasped her hands together. "The show, my dear friends, must go on!"

Aunt Cora thoughtfully considered the situation. "That's a fine offer, Arabella. One might even say a noble sacrifice. However, I have just one question for you. Do you know the part?"

"Do I know the part? Do *I* know the part?" Arabella cried. "Just listen!"

She dropped to her knees while the others stared. "O Romeo, Romeo, wherefore art thou Romeo?"

Arabella paused. She looked around the room, biting her lip. "Um, the rest slips my mind for the moment. I think it's something about love."

"That's a pretty safe guess," the doctor whispered to Christy.

"Arabella," Aunt Cora said patiently, "I know how much you want this part, dear. And maybe, if we had more time to prepare you. . . . But right now, we need someone who already knows all the lines. Someone who can learn the staging quickly, and be ready to go on opening night."

Arabella jumped to her feet. "And where exactly are you ever going to find someone like that?" she demanded.

It was a good question, Christy thought. A very good question.

Suddenly, she realized Aunt Cora was staring directly at her.

So was Doctor MacNeill.

And she had a very good idea what they were both thinking.

Ten

Christy!" Aunt Cora exclaimed.

"Christy," Doctor MacNeill said.

"Christy?" Oliver asked.

"Christy!" Gilroy cried.

"Christy?" Arabella screamed.

Christy took a step backward. All eyes were on her.

Aunt Cora looked hopeful. Doctor MacNeill looked encouraging. Oliver looked doubtful. Gilroy looked happy. Arabella looked shocked.

"Christy has performed the role of Juliet on stage," Aunt Cora said.

"In a high school gymnasium, Aunt Cora," Christy added quickly, "not on a real, professional stage."

"What's the difference?" Aunt Cora said. "An audience is an audience."

"B-but it was just an amateur production,"

Christy argued. "Halfway through the balcony scene, Romeo's little brother, Harry, jumped out of the audience, climbed onstage, and joined me in the balcony."

"And what did you do when Harry showed up?" Aunt Cora asked.

"I made up an extra line. I told Romeo I had to go because it was past my little brother's bedtime."

"The mark of a true professional!" Aunt Cora said. "The theater is always full of surprises. That's one of the reasons we love it so."

"I think Christy would make a lovely Juliet," Gilroy said.

"Told you he has a crush on you," the doctor whispered to Christy.

"But she's from Cutter Gap!" Arabella objected.

"So?" asked Gilroy.

"Well, we're the *Knoxville* Players, Gilroy."

Gilroy groaned. "I was born in Virginia, Arabella. This isn't about where you're from. It's about finding someone who can do the job."

"Gilroy is right," Aunt Cora agreed. "There are plenty of people in this room who know *some* of Juliet's lines. But there's only one person in this room who knows *all* of them."

"It isn't fair," Arabella pouted.

"Life isn't always fair, Arabella," Aunt Cora

said. "And speaking of fair, we haven't even asked Christy how she feels about all this."

A long pause followed. Everyone was waiting for Christy to respond. She tried to answer, but her mouth refused to make a sound.

See? a voice inside of her taunted. *You're tongue-tied in front of these people, Christy. It was one thing to play Juliet in front of your friends and family. It's quite another to perform in front of strangers in a professional theater.*

"I-I couldn't," Christy stuttered at last. "I mean, I'd love to help, I really would. But I just couldn't. I could do a walk-on part, maybe—one without any lines. I couldn't play Juliet."

"Christy, at least think about it," Aunt Cora began, but Christy didn't need to think about it. Her mind was made up. She quietly excused herself and went upstairs.

Behind her, she could hear Oliver's sad pronouncement: "I *told* you this play was doomed."

—◦— —◦—

Later that evening, there was a firm knock at Christy's bedroom door. "Christy? It's Neil. Did you find the party too boring?"

"It certainly wasn't boring." Christy opened the door.

The doctor leaned against the door jamb, arms crossed over his chest. "Everyone was sorry to see you go."

"Sorry," Christy shrugged. "I didn't know what else to do. I hated to let them all down, but I just can't do it, Neil. I was nervous enough about coming here and helping out in some small way. I didn't expect to be forced to take the starring role in a play."

"I understand. Aunt Cora said they may just cancel the play for the time being."

"Is she all right?"

"Oh, sure. She's a little disappointed, maybe." The doctor chuckled. "She's not as disappointed as Arabella, certainly."

Christy sighed. "Aunt Cora would be even more disappointed if I went out on stage, opened my mouth and nothing came out."

"Personally, I've never found you to be short of words."

"You don't understand. I don't even know if I remember all the lines, Neil! It's been a long time. And how do I know I wouldn't freeze up in front of all those people? Just stand there like a stone statue?"

"You don't. I guess you won't ever know unless you try." The doctor thought for a moment. "Seems to me you have to ask yourself if you'll look back on this moment someday and regret not having taken advantage of the opportunity. At least, that's what

Aunt Cora told me tonight, after I refused her offer of art lessons again."

"Why don't you try your hand at painting, Neil? If Aunt Cora knows a good teacher, this would be the perfect chance for you. It'd be a shame to pass it up . . ." Christy's voice trailed off. "I guess that sounds kind of silly coming from me, doesn't it?"

"I'll make you a deal," the doctor said. "I'll try my hand at painting, if you'll try your hand at playing Juliet. Just a day or two. No commitment."

Christy didn't answer. Her heart felt as if it were in her throat. She walked over to the window. Stars were scattered across the night sky, like glittering wildflowers in a field of endless black. Back home in Cutter Gap, her students might be looking up at this very sky right now—mischievous Creed, or gentle Little Burl, or fast-talking Ruby Mae.

What would they say, if she went back and told them about her adventure in Knoxville? How would they react, knowing their teacher had been too afraid to take a chance?

"You came all this way, Christy," the doctor said, joining her at the window, "Don't give up now."

Christy turned to him. "All right, then," she said at last, "but I want you to promise me something."

"Anything."

"If you get to see me perform as Juliet, then I get to see your very first painting."

"You drive a hard bargain, Christy Huddleston," the doctor said with a smile. He placed a soft kiss on her cheek. "It's a deal."

❧ Eleven ❧

"All right," Aunt Cora announced the next morning at the theater, "first things first. As most of you have heard by now, Christy has agreed to take on the demanding role of Juliet. For that, we are all very grateful."

"Hmmph," someone muttered.

Aunt Cora shot a warning look in Arabella's direction.

"Don't look at me!" Arabella cried. "I wish her nothing but the best."

"I want you all to be on your best behavior for the next few days," Aunt Cora continued. "Help show Christy the ropes. Make her feel at home. We've got a lot of ground to cover, and not much time. Christy, here's a copy of the play for you to look over. Use it the first couple of days of rehearsal to refresh your memory."

"Thank you," Christy said softly. "And I just want to tell everybody I'm grateful for this chance, and I'll do the very best I can. But please don't expect too much."

"You'll do just great." Gilroy patted her on the back. "If you got any questions, I'm the guy to ask. After all—" he winked, "I am Romeo."

"Later, we'll do a wardrobe fitting," Arabella said, eyeing Christy up and down. "I'll probably have to let out the costumes a bit," she said with the hint of a sneer.

"Whenever you say, Arabella," Christy said meekly.

"All right, people!" Aunt Cora clapped her hands. "I want to start this morning with act two, scene one. Romeo, Benvolio, Mercutio, let's get started." She turned to Christy. "Why don't you find yourself a nice, quiet spot to look over your lines? And don't hesitate to ask if you need anything."

What I really need is a dose of courage, Christy thought as she headed backstage. She almost wished the doctor were there for moral support. But today he was starting his art lessons, just as he'd promised.

In any case, it would probably have just made her more nervous to have Doctor MacNeill there, watching her stumble over her lines. He'd get to see her fail soon enough, on opening night. Assuming, that is, she lasted that long.

Christy found a wooden bench behind some props in an out-of-the-way corner of the stage. She got out her copy of the play and began to read through her lines.

"Hi, there."

Christy turned to see Marylou approaching. She was dressed in her dirty, paint-spattered overalls. A sprinkle of sawdust covered her hair.

"Hi, Marylou. What have you been up to?"

"A little of everything." Marylou shrugged shyly. "Sometimes I help with sets. Sometimes I do things for Oliver, when he starts to go crazy. Mostly, I help Ara-bellow." She grinned. "Oops. That's what we call her behind her back sometimes. It isn't very nice, I know."

"I imagine she can be rather difficult to work with."

"You're right about that." Marylou sat down on another bench. "So. You're going to be Juliet. Are you excited?"

"Scared, more than anything. But after talking it over with Doctor MacNeill last night, I decided I owed it to myself to give it a shot."

"You and Neil, you're pretty close?" Marylou asked carefully. "I saw you dancing at the party."

"He's a good friend, yes."

"You aim to marry him?"

Christy blushed at Marylou's rather blunt question. "I don't know about that . . ."

"No need to say anything. I can tell by the way you're gettin' all red that you're a little sweet on him."

Christy hesitated. She could feel her face burning.

"I figured as much," Marylou said. "Neil . . . well, he's quite a catch." She leapt off the bench. "Well, I have to get going. Ara-bellow wants me to help her mend some costumes."

"See you later," Christy called as Marylou dashed off. *He's quite a catch,* Marylou's words echoed in Christy's mind. Just how well did Marylou know Doctor MacNeill, anyway?

Christy looked down at her lines and sighed. It was going to be hard to concentrate, with all the chaos here. She'd have to do most of her practicing at Aunt Cora's, even if it meant staying up late into the night.

She turned to another scene and scanned the page. Nearby, Marylou's brother, Vernon, began hammering on a set.

Christy sighed again. It wasn't going to be hard to concentrate, she realized. It was going to be impossible.

━ ━ ━ ━

"Nice job, Christy!" Aunt Cora said that afternoon. "Very nice job!"

They'd practiced the same scene twice now, and both times, Christy had made a mess of her lines. Still, she'd gotten through the scene without thoroughly embarrassing herself, and that was something, at least.

"You're doing great," Gilroy whispered. "You're going to be the finest Juliet this theater's ever seen!"

"Thanks, Gilroy," Christy said. "Even if it's not true, it's nice to hear."

"You've got the bluest eyes I've ever seen," Gilroy said. "Except maybe for Marylou Marsh. I suppose you've got yourself lots of gentleman callers back home, huh?"

"Dozens and dozens," Christy said, but she realized from his expression that Gilroy thought she was serious. Before she could explain, Aunt Cora interrupted.

"Let's move on," she called from her front-row seat. "I want to get the staging squared away for act four, scene three, in Juliet's chamber. Christy, I want you to enter stage right. Don't worry about your lines right now. We just want to get the basic movements down. Move slowly across the stage until you reach the white bench, where you'll take your seat. Eventually, we'll have a bed there, too, but that's still being built. Got it?"

"That's simple enough that even I can handle it," Christy joked.

Christy made her way across the stage to the bench. She took her seat, trying her best to be graceful. In her head, she was reciting her lines, one by one. To her surprise, she remembered most of them.

"Fine," Aunt Cora said. "Now, after Lady Capulet enters and delivers her lines, I want you to stand and come three or four paces downstage."

Christy stood. Again, she silently recited her lines as she walked toward the edge of the stage.

Several people snickered. Christy hesitated. "Did I do something wrong?"

Gilroy pointed to her skirt. "It's your skirt, Christy. I guess the paint on that bench was still wet!"

Christy glanced over her shoulder. Sure enough, her favorite blue skirt was covered with paint.

"That bench was painted two weeks ago!" Aunt Cora cried. "How could it still be wet?"

"Someone must have put a second coat on," Arabella suggested. She strode over to Christy's side. "We professionals know to check for such things," she said. "Come on. I'll see if I can find something you can change into."

"Sorry about that, dear. Welcome to the theater," Aunt Cora said with a laugh. "I told you it's full of surprises!"

❧ Twelve ❧

How was your first day of rehearsal?" Doctor MacNeill asked that evening at dinner.

"Humbling," Christy replied.

"She was magnificent. A natural," Aunt Cora said as she passed Christy a loaf of warm bread. "I was very proud of her."

"Aunt Cora's just being nice. I couldn't remember half my lines. I stumbled over the other half. And to top it all off, I sat on a bench covered with wet paint and ruined my skirt."

"I feel so terrible about that," Aunt Cora said. "It's the strangest thing. That paint should have been dry as a bone. But as I told you, these things happen. Before you leave Knoxville, I'll take you shopping and we'll buy you a new skirt."

"Don't be silly, Aunt Cora. It doesn't matter. I'm just sorry I'm not doing a better job for you."

"You're not quitting already, are you?" Doctor MacNeill shook his fork at Christy. "Because if you quit, then I'm definitely quitting my art lessons."

"Didn't you enjoy yourself today, Neil?" Aunt Cora asked.

"Let's just say if I were as bad a doctor as I am a painter, I wouldn't have a patient left alive."

Christy laughed. "Neil, it's only your first day. Give it time."

"I was going to say the same thing to you."

"All right, then," Christy agreed. "Another day or two. Now, if you two will excuse me, I've got some lines to go memorize."

"I'm always available to fill in as Romeo," the doctor offered.

Christy grinned. "I'll keep that in mind."

<hr />

The next morning at rehearsal, Christy waited in the large dressing room backstage while Aunt Cora rehearsed with some of the other actors. Christy was so busy working on her lines that she barely noticed the small figure reflected in the mirror.

"Oliver?" she asked, spinning around.

"I'm sorry to disturb you," he muttered. "I left my hat in here the other day, when I departed in such a huff."

"I thought you were wearing one at the party."

"A different hat," he snapped. He poked around in a pile of costumes. "No matter. It's not as if anyone cares whether my head is warm. I'm sure they'd all be thrilled if I caught cold and expired."

"Oliver, don't say that. I can tell the cast is very fond of you. I think the pressure was just getting to everyone."

"*Fond!* Phooey! They hate me, all of them. And of course they *love* Cora. Sure, Cora is the perfect director. All I heard while she was away was, 'Why can't you be more like Cora, Oliver?' Well, I'm not Cora! I'm Oliver! Oliver Flump!"

"Of course you are."

He sighed. The anger seemed to vanish. "But you like her, too, no doubt. Sweet, patient Cora."

"I do. I think she's a wonderful director. But I'm sure you would be, too—in your own way."

"She'll get her comeuppance, soon enough."

"What do you mean?" Christy asked, frowning.

"I mean this play will fall apart at the seams, and *then* we'll see who the true director is!"

"Because of me, you mean? You mean the play will fall apart because I'm taking the role of Juliet?"

Oliver patted her gently on the shoulder. "It's not your fault, my dear. It's Cora's. If she had left me in charge, things would be different. I could have gotten the actors under control. Discipline, that's what they need—a firm hand."

"I hope I don't ruin everything," Christy said forlornly.

"You won't ruin the play, Christy. Fate will. And when that happens, everyone will recognize my true genius." Oliver buttoned his topcoat. "Well, I must be off. I'm not wanted here."

Christy watched him go. She couldn't help feeling a little resentful. She was having a hard enough time keeping her confidence up. Oliver wasn't helping matters with his gloomy predictions.

"Christy!" Arabella poked her head in the door. Her strong perfume filled the room. "Cora's calling for you."

"Here I come," Christy said, but as she stood up, a horrible ripping sound met her ears.

Arabella clucked her tongue. "I *knew* that skirt was a little tight on you."

"But . . ." Christy took another step, and her skirt ripped some more. A large patch of fabric was stuck to the chair.

"It's glued!" Christy cried. "Somebody glued my chair!"

"Don't be absurd," Arabella sniffed. "Why would anybody . . ." She examined the chair. "Sure enough." She tapped a finger on her chin. "Goodness, this *is* unfortunate. I'm not sure I've got another spare skirt."

"Well, I can't go out on stage with my petticoat showing," Christy said frantically.

"Let me see what I can rustle up. You stay put."

A few minutes later, Arabella returned. She was carrying something shiny and stiff. It looked like a pair of men's trousers, made of metal.

"What on earth is that?" Christy asked.

"Armor. From our last play, *Joan of Arc*. I think it'll fit you nicely."

"I can't wear that, Arabella!"

"Well, it's not the whole suit of armor, just the bottom. Think of it as a very well-starched pair of pants."

Christy crossed her arms over her chest. "This is ridiculous. There must be something else I can—"

"Christy!" Marylou appeared at the door. "You'd better hurry! Everybody's waitin'!"

"When there's a crisis in the theater, we all do our part," Arabella told Christy. "You must try to be cooperative."

"Oh, all right. I'll wear it. But I'm going to look completely ridiculous."

"I'm sure you'll look rather . . . charming," Arabella said.

Moments later, Christy clunked her way onto the stage. Her armor-covered legs were so stiff she could barely move. She was greeted with gales of laughter.

"Interesting fashion choice," said Aunt Cora, grinning. "But I don't think it's quite Juliet's style."

"My dress ripped," Christy said sullenly. She didn't think there was any point in explaining *how* it had ripped. If a practical joker had deliberately put glue on her chair, she didn't want to give that person the satisfaction of seeing her upset.

"Well, let's proceed. We've got a lot to cover today. Let's start with the scene in Capulet's orchard."

Aunt Cora pointed to a group of wooden trees in the center of the stage. They were five tall pieces of wood, cut and painted to resemble apple trees. A wooden stand at the base kept each tree erect.

"Juliet—I mean, Christy—you'll enter first from stage left, followed by the nurse."

Christy did as she was told. *Clank. Clank. Clank.* Every step made a horrible noise, but Christy was determined to struggle on. Behind her, she could hear the whispers and giggles of her fellow cast members.

"Fine. Stop there," Aunt Cora directed. "Now, let's hear your lines. Try to direct your voice even farther than yesterday. This is an awfully big theater, so you need to project."

Christy cleared her throat. "Gallop apace, you fiery-footed steeds—" she began.

"Even louder, dear," Aunt Cora called.

"Gallop apace, you fiery-footed—"

"Look out!" someone yelled.

Suddenly, as if in slow motion, the apple tree behind Christy began to fall. Christy lurched sideways, out of its path. The movement was too sudden for her metal-clad legs.

There was no way to regain her balance. With a horrible thud, Christy landed on her backside, as the apple tree toppled to the floor, only inches away.

"Christy! Are you all right?" Gilroy ran to her side.

"I'm fine. Although this is my worst nightmare come true," Christy admitted with a shaky laugh.

"It'd be worse with a full house," Gilroy pointed out.

"I want somebody to explain to me what just happened," Aunt Cora said sternly.

One of the stagehands examined the tree. "There's a rope attached to the bottom of this prop tree. Somebody must have yanked on it. I'm awful sorry, Christy."

"Don't worry about it," Christy said. "I'm fine. However, it may take the entire cast to help me stand up in this armor."

"I feel terrible about this," Aunt Cora said. "Here you are, doing your best to help us out, and somebody's pulling these silly pranks."

"I'll say one thing. I'm starting to get the feeling somebody doesn't want me to star in this play," Christy said with a grim smile.

❧ Thirteen ❧

I wish I could get to the bottom of this, Christy," Aunt Cora apologized, "but I still haven't got a clue about who's sabotaging this play."

Four days had passed. Christy had endured several more pranks, each one more embarrassing than the last.

"What we need is a motive," said Doctor MacNeill.

He had set up an easel in Aunt Cora's parlor and was painting his first picture. Aunt Cora and Christy were seated on the far side of the room. Nobody was allowed to see the doctor's work—at least, not yet.

"Well, since most of the pranks have been directed at me, my first choice would be Arabella," Christy said. "You have to admit, she seems awfully jealous about my getting the part of Juliet."

"In all honesty, Christy," Aunt Cora said, "I wouldn't be surprised if several of the other cast members are a little jealous of you. Not that they're being fair, but acting can be very competitive."

"Still, Arabella always seems to be around when something goes wrong."

"Of course, you could say that about any of the cast," Aunt Cora observed. "They've all been present."

"Even Oliver," Christy said. "I've seen him lurking about every single day—although he keeps a low profile."

"I knew he wouldn't be able to keep away. He lives and breathes the theater."

The doctor stepped back to examine his work, his paintbrush in midair. "Perhaps you should consider Oliver a suspect. He has a motive, too."

"He does seem very upset about not getting to direct," Christy said. "He was even predicting all kinds of bad things were going to happen."

Aunt Cora just laughed. "Oh, that's just Oliver. He predicts dire things every day of his life. It's just his way. He's a born pessimist."

"Well, all I know is, I've suffered through wet paint, a falling tree, glue-ruined clothes, chairs collapsing when I went to sit in them, and a large beetle magically appearing in my ham sandwich."

"In all fairness, that may have been the beetle's idea," Doctor MacNeill said.

"Watch what you say, Neil," Christy warned, "or I'll come over there and look at your painting!"

"My masterpiece?" the doctor cried. "No one can see this until it's ready. And if I have my way, it'll *never* be ready!"

"I don't know what else to do, Christy," said Aunt Cora, wringing her hands. "I've spoken to everyone individually. I've scolded the whole group. This isn't the first time they've pulled practical jokes on new cast members, but it's definitely the worst. I just feel so awful."

"Don't. It's not your fault."

Aunt Cora checked the clock on the mantel. "Listen, I need to run a quick errand. You two sit tight. I'll be right back."

"Would you like some company?" Christy asked.

"No, no. You stay put. You've been working so hard." Aunt Cora smiled at the doctor. "We're having a surprise for dinner, by the way."

"Maybe I could help—" Christy began.

"I won't hear of it. Besides, this is my secret recipe. I think it will add a little down-home flavor you'll like."

"Sounds interesting," Christy said.

"Oh, I think it will definitely be interesting."

Christy walked Aunt Cora to the door, then returned to the parlor. "Neil, I didn't want to say anything in front of Aunt Cora, but I'm starting to wonder if maybe I should pull out of the play."

"Pull out! But you can't!" Doctor MacNeill tossed aside his paintbrush and joined Christy on the sofa. "You've been doing so well, Christy. You said so yourself. Just yesterday you were talking about how much more confident you felt on stage."

"Acting, yes. But how can I really relax when I keep waiting for the next practical joke? Somebody wants me out of that play, Neil. That's all there is to it."

"You know, at least some of those pranks affected other people. When that rolled-up curtain fell onto the stage yesterday, you and Gilroy were both there. And several people were near you when that other set toppled."

"I know. But I think that's just coincidence. I do seem to be the main target."

Christy walked over to the wall where Aunt Cora had her theater posters displayed. "I keep thinking about what Miss Alice told me. About how I should ask myself what the worst thing that could happen would be. I *thought* it would be falling on the stage in front of people. Well, I've done that, and then some."

"But you're still worried?"

Christy touched one of the framed posters and sighed. "I'm afraid something even worse may happen opening night. I might even get hurt. Lots of people might."

"Maybe you're right to be worried," the doctor said, joining her. He gave her a gentle hug. "I've been making light of all this because Aunt Cora said the actors often initiate new cast members with practical jokes. But if you're afraid, I think you should pull out. They can always do the play next year."

"I'd hate to disappoint everyone. Especially Aunt Cora. But I'm starting to feel like it's my only choice."

"Maybe if you give it another day—"

"Neil, the show's in two days. I need to make a decision soon." Christy started for the dining room. "In the meantime, if Aunt Cora's making us a special dinner, the least I can do is set the table."

"Want help?"

"No. You stay and finish your masterpiece."

While she set the table, Christy practiced what she would say to Aunt Cora. *I'm sorry, Aunt Cora, but I just can't take the risk of performing. Maybe some other time. Maybe some other role . . .*

But of course, there would be no other

role. This was her chance. Her one big chance.

Christy was just setting the last plate into place when she heard the front door open. "Aunt Cora?" she called, but nobody answered.

She heard loud whispers, followed by a shrill giggle.

Christy headed toward the hall. "Aunt Cora, is that you?"

"It's us, Miz Christy!" a childish voice cried.

Christy turned the corner and stared in disbelief.

There in the hall stood Aunt Cora, along with what looked like half the population of Cutter Gap.

"Ruby Mae!" Christy cried. "Creed! Little Burl! Miss Alice!" She counted eleven students, plus Miss Alice.

"Aunt Cora done paid for our tickets so we could come and see you actin'!" Creed explained.

"I made arrangements with Miss Alice before I left Cutter Gap," Aunt Cora said. "Of course, then I thought you'd only have a small walk-on role!"

"I can't believe you're all here," Christy whispered.

"I would have arranged for the whole cove to come if I could have," Aunt Cora said. "But there just plain wasn't room. So the children drew lots to see who would come."

"David felt he could spare me for a couple days," Miss Alice said, rushing to give Christy a hug. "We're all so proud of you, Christy."

"But I was going to—" Christy began. "Aunt Cora, I really don't know . . ."

"No need to thank me, dear," Aunt Cora said breezily. "It'll be all the thanks I need when I see your friends applauding in their front-row seats!"

❧ Fourteen ❧

Well, look at you, Teacher! All gussied up so fancy-like!" Ruby Mae exclaimed the following afternoon.

The dressing room was filled to overflowing with Christy's friends from Cutter Gap. They'd just returned from a tour of the theater with Aunt Cora. She'd brought them to the dressing room to see Christy in her "Juliet finery," as Ruby Mae called it.

"You look just like a fairy princess, Miz Christy," Creed pronounced. "But how come your lips are so all-fired red?"

"That's makeup, Creed," Aunt Cora explained. "All the actors wear makeup. It's easier for the people in the audience to see their faces that way."

"Christy, are you certain you don't mind having all of us in the audience for the dress rehearsal today?" Miss Alice asked.

"I might as well get used to having a real audience," Christy said gamely. *Since it looks like I'm going through with this, after all*, she added to herself. "Let's just hope nothing goes wrong today."

"I'm sure everyone will be on their best behavior," Aunt Cora said. "After all, we open tomorrow. I doubt you'll have any more trouble with your prankster."

Arabella poked her head in the door. "I see the costume fits," she said, smiling at Christy's flowing blue gown.

"I'm all set, except that I can't seem to locate those shoes I was supposed to wear," Christy said. "I've looked everywhere."

"Let me scout around," Arabella said. "You go on ahead."

While her Cutter Gap friends gathered in the audience, Christy joined her fellow actors onstage.

"Nervous?" Gilroy asked.

Christy nodded. "I seem to have swallowed a hundred butterflies."

"I get that way, too, a little," Gilroy admitted. "'Course, I'm even worse around girls I like. I get so nervous, I just start jabbering like a jaybird. Like when I'm around Marylou, for instance."

"Gilbert, do you have a crush on Marylou?"

"She isn't easy to talk to, like you are. But she does have the most beautiful smile. . . ."

88

Gilroy shrugged. "Lately, this past week or so, she won't even give me the time of day. I guess she has her eye on some other fella."

"Where is Marylou, anyway?"

"Running around like a chicken with her head cut off." Gilbert grinned. "Ol' Ara-bellow keeps her hopping."

Just then, Oliver tapped Christy on the shoulder. It was the first time he'd made an appearance backstage, although she'd seen him several times, watching the play from one of the rear seats.

"Oliver!" she exclaimed.

"I just wanted to wish you the best," he said. "I expect you'll need it, the way things have been going. So as we say in the theater, break a leg, my dear." He chuckled to himself. "Plenty of other things have certainly been breaking around here."

Just then, Arabella appeared, carrying the black leather ballet slippers Christy was supposed to wear with her costume. "Here you go, dear," she said, placing the slippers on the floor. "By the way, you look simply lovely."

"Thanks, Arabella." Christy eased her left foot into the slipper. "It really is a beautiful cos—"

"Is something wrong?" Arabella inquired.

"There's something in my slipper! It . . . it feels sort of . . ."

Christy curled her nose. A smell—a horrible, stomach-turning stench was filling the air.

Instantly, she knew what it was—the smell of a rotten egg.

"What *is* that appalling odor?" Arabella pinched her nose. "Christy, don't be offended, but is that *you*, dear?"

Christy pulled off her shoe, revealing the gooey remains of an egg.

"I think you know what that smell is, Arabella! You're the one who brought me the slippers. It's pretty easy to figure out that you're the one who put the egg there!"

"I did no such thing!" Arabella cried indignantly. "Where would someone of my stature get a rotten egg?"

"Would somebody *please* tell me what that vile smell is?" Aunt Cora called from her seat in the front row.

"Can you smell it down there?" Gilroy asked, waving his hand in front of his face.

"They could smell that odor in California," Aunt Cora said.

"Somebody put a rotten egg in my shoe!" Christy cried. She felt hot tears forming, but willed them to stop.

Aunt Cora leapt to her feet. "This whole thing has gone quite far enough!" she yelled. "I want whoever is behind this to step forward right this instant!"

Christy glared at Arabella.

"I had nothing to do with this, I'm telling you!" Arabella said. "Why, the smell is making me positively faint!"

Christy turned to Oliver.

"I said, 'Break a leg,'" he said. "Not 'Break an egg.'"

Christy surveyed the rest of her fellow cast members. They all seemed to be looking at her with complete sympathy. But that didn't matter. One of these people was trying to hurt and embarrass her. And she'd had enough.

"That does it," Christy said. "I am nervous enough about this without having to be afraid a prop's going to fall on me. I'm tired of being humiliated this way."

"Christy," Gilroy said, "you know we're all behind you."

"Most of you are, I know. But I've made my decision, Gilroy. I am not going out on stage tomorrow night. You'll just have to cancel the play."

≈ Fifteen ≈

I just can't help feeling like I've let every-one down," Christy said.

It was evening, and Christy was sitting in Aunt Cora's parlor with her friends from Cutter Gap. A fire crackled in the fireplace. Outside, light rain trickled down the windowpanes.

"Nonsense, Christy." Aunt Cora squeezed her hand. "We all understand."

"But the cast and crew . . . all their hard work will go down the drain." Christy leaned back in her chair and sighed. "Yours, too, Aunt Cora. Plus, I'll be disappointing all these friends who came from Cutter Gap just to see me."

"Don't you fret none, Miz Christy," said Creed. "We got to ride a train and we got to stay in Aunt Cora's fancy house. And we got to step inside a real, live theater."

"Creed's right," said Ruby Mae in a comforting voice. "That's plenty of fun for us. 'Course, we *was* a-hopin' to see you actin' up a storm as Juliet."

"I was, too, Ruby Mae," said Christy. "But you all understand, don't you? How could I go out on that stage tomorrow night, knowing something awful could go wrong? It was bad enough when I was just afraid I'd forget my lines or fall down. Now I have to be afraid it will start raining rotten eggs during the balcony scene. And what if someone got hurt?"

"That sure would be a sight to behold!" said Little Burl.

Christy managed a smile. "Back at the theater I felt certain I'd made the right decision. But now, I feel lousy about it. So many people were counting on me."

"You know, the theater is a little like life, isn't it?" Miss Alice reflected.

"Like Shakespeare said: 'All the world's a stage,'" Aunt Cora quoted.

"It seems to me that in our lives we can't always predict what will happen," Miss Alice said. "People get sick. Or they lose their jobs. Or bad weather strikes . . ."

"We've certainly seen our share of those things in Cutter Gap," said Doctor MacNeill. "We've had typhoid, poverty, and floods."

"But the way we get from one day to the next is to have faith that if we trust in God to help us, we can triumph over any adversity," Miss Alice said. She smiled. "Even over a storm of rotten eggs."

Christy looked at the hopeful, innocent faces of her students. She knew what Miss Alice was saying. She meant that this was Christy's chance to teach the children something far more valuable than any grammar or spelling lesson.

"Aunt Cora," Christy said firmly, "call the cast. I'm going to go through with this play, after all. Eggs or no eggs."

"Miz Christy!" Little Burl cried. "You're a-goin' to be Juliet, after all?"

"I'm going to try, Little Burl."

Aunt Cora hugged her close. "You won't regret this, I promise. I'll have the cast keep such a close watch on you, there won't be a chance for anyone to pull another prank."

"I'll be fine, no matter what," Christy said. "Miss Alice is right. I just have to have faith."

"Are you for sure and certain, Miz Christy?" Ruby Mae asked doubtfully.

"For sure and certain. I promise I won't change my mind again. I can't let one person ruin the play for everyone else."

"Was that the front door?" Aunt Cora asked.

"I'll get it," Ruby Mae volunteered.

A moment later, she returned with Marylou. "Hello, everybody," Marylou said softly.

"Marylou! What brings you here?" said Doctor MacNeill.

"Hello, Neil." Marylou smiled shyly. "I just came to bring Christy her coat." She handed it to Christy. "I guess you left it in the dressing room today."

"I was in a bit of a hurry," Christy said. "Thanks, Marylou."

"What a sweet girl, to come out in this rain!" Miss Alice exclaimed.

"I didn't mind. I wanted to come and say a proper goodbye to Christy and Neil . . ." Marylou cast a quick glance in his direction. "I guess you'll be leavin' now, what with the play canceled and all. I just want you to know I feel right bad about the way things turned out."

"Actually, there's been a change in plans. I've decided to go through with the play, after all."

"You have?" Marylou asked, clearly surprised. She hesitated. "Well, that's really good news, Christy. Yes, it is."

"Marylou, maybe you could help me get in touch with the cast and crew," Aunt Cora said.

"Sure. I'd be happy to."

Aunt Cora smiled gratefully. "You've been such a great help during this play, Marylou."

"Thank you."

"I left the cast list in the kitchen. I'll get it and we can divide up the names between us," Aunt Cora said.

"Bye, Neil. I guess you'll be there tomorrow?" Marylou asked.

"I wouldn't miss it for the world." He patted Christy's shoulder. "I intend to have a front-row seat for Christy's debut."

"You might want to reconsider where you sit. There's always the danger you'll be pelted by rotten eggs," Christy warned.

"I'll take my chances," the doctor said.

"Miz Christy? Would you help me brush these snarls outa my hair?" Ruby Mae asked that evening. "It's so tangled up I'm afeared I'll pull my whole head off if'n I tug any harder."

"Sure." Carefully, Christy began to brush through Ruby Mae's wild, red hair.

"I'm awful glad you decided to be Juliet," Ruby Mae said, wincing slightly.

"Me too—I think."

"When I grow up, I might just be an actress, too."

"You'd be good at it," Christy said with an affectionate smile. "You certainly know how to act like you've done your homework when you really haven't."

Ruby Mae ignored the remark. "That gal

who came with your coat today. What part does she play?"

"Marylou? She works behind the scenes, helping the director and the costume designer." Christy tugged on a particularly tough tangle. "Sorry. I have to pull a little. You know, Marylou and the doctor were friends when they were younger."

"Sweethearts?"

"I doubt it," Christy replied. "She used to beat him up every chance she got!"

Ruby Mae laughed. "Oh, they was sweethearts for sure, then."

"Why do you say that?"

"Well, when *I* was a little 'un, I used to beat up on boys regular as could be when I was sweet on 'em."

Christy stopped brushing. "You mean it was a sign of affection?"

"Oh, yes'm. Nothin' serious, mind you. No broken bones or nothin'. Just wrasslin'."

"Really?"

"Sure. If I didn't like 'em, why would I have bothered to take the time to whop 'em so good?"

Christy considered for a moment. "Ruby Mae," she said, nodding, "I believe you've just provided me with a very interesting clue."

❧ Sixteen ❧

"Two and a half hours till show time," Aunt Cora said to Christy the following evening. "How are you holding up?"

"I'm a nervous wreck," Christy admitted. She was sitting patiently in the dressing room while Arabella applied Christy's stage makeup.

"Try not to move your mouth," Arabella grumbled.

"Don't worry, Christy. You're supposed to be a nervous wreck," Aunt Cora said. "It goes with the territory." She headed for the door. "I've got to go make sure the programs are here. Anything you need?"

"Just a dose of courage."

"Nonsense, you've got plenty to spare."

Arabella stood back, staring at Christy critically. "A little more rouge, I think," she murmured. "You may need a touch-up later, by the way. I don't know why you insisted on getting ready so early. You're practically the first cast member here tonight."

"I have something I need to do before the show starts," Christy replied.

"Well, just don't muss up my fine handiwork." Arabella dabbed some pink color on Christy's cheeks. "There. The perfect Juliet. Thanks, in no small part, to me."

"Arabella," Christy said softly, "I want to apologize for accusing you about the rotten egg. It was wrong of me, and I'm sorry."

"Apology accepted. We all get a bit cranky sometimes. And I know you're under a lot of pressure." She tucked a wisp of hair behind Christy's ear. "But don't worry, darling. You're going to knock 'em dead."

"Thanks, Arabella."

When Arabella left, Christy stared at her reflection in the big mirror on the wall. "O Romeo, Romeo, wherefore art thou Romeo?" she whispered.

Her voice was trembling. So were her hands. Two and half hours till the curtain rose, and already she was so nervous she could barely whisper her lines. How would she ever make it through the night?

With a sigh, Christy climbed out of her chair. There was no point in feeling sorry for herself. She had work to do. She was going to try to keep this play from being sabotaged. And she didn't have much time.

— — —

Fifteen minutes had passed. The backstage area was still practically deserted. After this afternoon's final rehearsal, most of the cast had headed home to rest before the show.

But if someone was planning on sabotaging the play, Christy reasoned, they'd probably show up early to set things up. Why would they risk getting caught closer to show time? By then, everybody would be on the lookout for the person who'd been causing all the trouble.

Christy leaned against a wall and sighed. Maybe she should give up. There was no sign of Marylou—or of anyone else, for that matter.

Just as she turned down a hallway, Christy noticed Marylou's younger brother, Vernon, stepping into the storage area where the costumes were kept. He closed the door behind him.

Christy tiptoed down the hall and put her ear to the door. Carefully, she turned the door handle and opened the door a crack.

Vernon's back was to the door. He was in the far corner of the dimly-lit room. A lamplight flickered. Huge shadows danced on the wall.

Christy watched in shock as he pulled her costume off a rack and turned the gown inside-out.

Gently, slowly, Christy eased into the room and slipped behind a rack of costumes.

Vernon didn't seem to notice. He pulled a metal can out of his pocket and opened the top. Then he upended the can and began shaking it over Christy's costume. Out rained a fine powder.

Suddenly, the door flew open.

"Vernon!" Marylou cried. "What are you doing? I told you no more, and I meant it!"

"B—but Marylou! What's the point, if we don't do something tonight, of all nights? I thought you *wanted* me to do this."

"Not anymore." Marylou sighed. "After I went over to Cora's yesterday, I could see the way Neil was lookin' at Christy. I realized he's never goin' to look at me that way, Vernon. Most likely, no fella ever will."

Christy stepped out from behind the rack of clothes.

"Sakes alive!" Vernon cried, leaping backward. The can of powder dropped to the floor.

"You've been behind this whole thing, haven't you, Marylou?" Christy asked, trying to rein in her fury.

Marylou's shoulders slumped. "Yes. And I'm awful sorry, Christy, not that sayin' so does much good now. I was just . . . hurtin', I suppose."

"You mean because you've always had a crush on Neil?"

"For as long as I can remember. And then, when he came back to Knoxville, saying how we ought to get together and all, and then nothing came of it. . . . Besides, I could see you were sweet on each other." She wiped away a tear. "I've got no excuse, Christy."

"So you recruited Vernon to help you set up your tricks?"

Vernon grinned proudly. "I came up with this one all on my own!"

"What's in the can, Vernon?" Christy asked.

"Itchin' powder."

Marylou groaned. "I *told* him no more. I started thinkin' on how sad everyone was goin' to be, if the play was canceled. Even ol' Ara-bellow."

"I couldn't help myself," Vernon said with a giggle. "It was such a fine trick, don't you see?"

Christy managed a smile. "Yes, it certainly was ingenious, Vernon. Only now what am I going to do?"

"Maybe we could wash off the powder," Marylou suggested.

"Nope." Vernon shook his head. "It sticks like glue. That was my doin', too, by the way," he added proudly. "Remember the glue on the chair?"

"You're quite the mischief-maker, Vernon," Christy said. "I've got a couple of students just like you."

Marylou thumbed through the racks of clothes. "I've got it!" she said. "Although it may take a little work." She pulled out a long, pale green dress.

"It looks like my gown," Christy said. "But it's about three sizes too big."

"Not by the time I'm done with it. We've got two hours. And nobody stitches faster than I do."

"Do you really think you can do it?"

"You just wait, Christy. I'll have this dress ready for you before you know it!" Marylou paused. "But there's just one condition."

"Yes?"

"You promise to forgive me for the rotten way I've been actin'."

Christy gave her a hug. "Of course I forgive you. By the way, you're wrong about one thing."

"What's that?"

"You said no fellow would ever look at you the way Neil looks at me. But I know that a member of the cast has a secret crush on you."

"You're just pullin' my leg."

"Nope," Christy smiled. "It just so happens he goes by the name of Romeo."

❧ Seventeen ❧

There's a full house," Christy whispered, peeking out from behind the heavy, velvet curtain.

"I still don't understand why you changed your costume at the last minute like this," Arabella muttered. "It's very unprofessional. Besides, pale green will completely clash with my set."

"It'll match my complexion perfectly," Christy joked.

Aunt Cora signaled Christy. "Get ready for your entrance, Juliet," she whispered.

Christy took a deep breath. She closed her eyes.

She knew the play as if she'd written it herself. She knew the set as if she'd been born there. She knew her character as if she really *were* Juliet.

It was time.

Christy stepped onto the stage.

Her throat tightened. Her heart raced.

What was her first line? She couldn't remember her line!

See? a voice inside of her taunted. *You're not ready for this, Christy. You're going to fail. You're doomed.*

Christy gazed out into the audience at the vast sea of faces.

She could feel her fellow actors waiting, holding their breath, crossing their fingers.

With God's help, I know I can do this, Christy told herself.

She closed her eyes and silently prayed. When Christy opened her eyes, she glanced down at the front row. Miss Alice was there, and so were Christy's students.

But for now, they weren't her students.

For now, the audience wasn't there.

For a few moments, while the magic of the theater lasted, her name would be Juliet, and the stage would be hers.

❦ ❦ ❦

"A stunning performance," Doctor MacNeill told Christy that evening at the cast party.

"Maybe not stunning," Christy said, "but it sure was fun! Once I started acting, I actually had a good time."

"Miz Christy," Creed tugged on Christy's arm, "could I have your writin' name?"

"My writin' name?"

"He means your autograph," Ruby Mae explained, nudging Creed out of the way. "First, sign my program, Miz Christy."

"No, mine!" Creed yelped.

"Write on mine, Teacher!" Bessie demanded.

"Suddenly, I don't feel like a star anymore." Christy winked at the doctor. "I feel like a teacher."

"You ain't a-goin' to run off and be an actor for good, are you?" Creed asked nervously.

"No, Creed. Acting's fun. But teaching's my real love."

Just as Christy had finished signing the programs, Oliver came over. "A class act!" he cried. "I knew you were a class act the minute I laid eyes on you!" He bowed and kissed her hand.

"Why, Oliver!" Christy said.

"You didn't have to invite me on stage for that last curtain call," Oliver said. "Not after the way I've been acting. But it was a real honor to share the stage with such a pro. Now, if you'll excuse me, I've got business to discuss with Cora. I'm hoping she'll let me direct our *next* play . . ."

"That was awfully thoughtful of you," the doctor said.

"He's a sweet man," Christy said, "even if

he *can* be a little difficult." She pulled the doctor aside. "By the way, you and I had a deal. Fair is fair. It's time for you to unveil your painting."

The doctor groaned. "I was hoping you'd forget."

"Not on your life."

"Come on, then. It's over in the corner, covered by a sheet. Just don't let anybody else see it."

Before he removed the covering, Doctor MacNeill held up a warning finger. "Don't forget this is my first effort."

"I understand. Let me guess—I'll bet it's a painting of the mountains. The view from your cabin porch."

"Not exactly. Although my goal *was* to capture the beauty of the place." Suddenly, he dropped the sheet. "I can't. It's too awful. It doesn't even begin to do my subject justice."

"Neil—" Christy grabbed the sheet, "let me see—"

She pulled back the sheet and gasped. A smile came to her lips. "It's . . . it's . . . me!"

"Not even close to you," the doctor said. To Christy's surprise, he was blushing. "I mean, the nose is all wrong. And the mouth. And look at your ears! They look like elephant ears! You have wonderful ears, and I made you look like a circus animal!"

"Neil." Christy placed a gentle kiss on his

cheek. "It's wonderful. It's the most beautiful painting I've ever seen, because it came from the artist's heart. May I keep it?"

"You really want it?"

"I'd be honored to have it."

"But the ears—"

"Never mind the ears."

"All right, then," the doctor said. "But next time I paint your portrait, I'm getting the ears right."

"It's rather a mysterious smile," Christy observed.

The doctor nodded. "That's because I still haven't unlocked the secrets of your heart. Of course, if you'd let me have a peek at that diary of yours . . ."

"Don't count on it," Christy said.

~ ~ ~

That night, after everyone else was fast asleep, Christy got out her diary and pen.

She didn't want the magic of the evening to be lost, not ever. Somehow, she felt if she wrote down the right words, she'd be able to preserve the thrill forever:

> *It's very late, and I know I should be asleep. But it's as if the excitement of tonight is still with me—the applause, the bows, the bouquet of roses from the cast.*

But the strange thing is, while it was wonderful to live out my fantasy of appearing on stage, that isn't what I'll take away with me from this night.

What matters most to me is that I faced my fear and rose above it. I had faith that with God's help I could get through a difficult time. And I was right.

But now, looking back, I can see that it was just a small fear. The important thing is that I can apply what I've learned to other challenges—harder tasks and bigger fears. As long as I remember to try my hardest and trust in God, there's no telling what I may accomplish!

❧ Eighteen ❧

Sorry, folks. It's time for your spelling test," Christy announced, "whether you're ready or not."

A week had passed. Christy was back in Cutter Gap. Everything had returned to normal. Under David's watchful eye, the children had kept up with their lessons. After a couple of days of excitement following Christy's return, everyone had settled down.

Even for Christy, the adventure in Knoxville now seemed like a dream. It was hard to believe she'd actually set foot on that big stage—let alone that she'd taken repeated bows to thunderous applause.

"Take out your blackboards, children," Christy said. "I'm sure if you studied, you won't have any trouble with these words."

"Miz Christy?" Creed frantically waved his hand. "I got an idea."

Christy put her hands on her hips. "You've stalled as long as you can, Creed. It's time to face the music."

"How about if we do some rememberin' about goin' to Knoxville first?" Creed pleaded.

"We've done that. Repeatedly. You got to show everyone your program. We talked about what it was like to ride on a train. Bessie showed us her drawing of Aunt Cora's house. And Ruby Mae did a fine impression of me on the stage as Juliet. Don't you think we've relived Knoxville enough for one week?"

Creed sighed. "I s'pose so," he said, his face downcast. "But I just wanted to tell everybody about one more thing."

Christy had seen Creed pull this trick a dozen times—always right before a big test. But he'd looked so disappointed, she decided to relent this time.

"All right. One more thing."

Creed stood up so that everyone could hear him. "I just wanted to tell about what it was like the night of the big play."

The class fell into rapt attention. Although there had been a little jealousy from the children who hadn't been lucky enough to go to Knoxville, they never seemed to tire of hearing stories about what it had been like. Perhaps, Christy reflected, because they hoped someday they, too, would get the chance for an adventure of their own.

"The thing of it is," Creed continued, "when Miz Christy walked out onto that stage for the first time, she looked just like a fairy princess in one of those stories she's always a-tellin' us. But the best part was, she was *my* teacher, my very own! I knowed she was afeared about goin' out there, what with all the pranks and such. And there she was, sure as shootin', only she wasn't just Teacher anymore."

Ruby Mae nodded. "Nope," she said softly, "she was Juliet!"

"I tell you," Creed said, "I thought my chest was goin' to split right open, with all the pride I was feelin'!"

Listening to Creed, Christy knew with all her heart that *this* was the real stage where she belonged. This was a much tougher audience, to be sure. But their applause was what really mattered.

"Thank you, Creed," she said. "That was very sweet. But you know when I feel the most pride? When I look out at all of you and realize I'm helping you learn and grow."

Creed raised his hand again. "Miz Christy? I got another bit of tellin' to do—"

Christy laughed. "Nice try, Creed. But you can't stall forever. Maybe later, we can do some more telling. Right now, it's time for some *spelling*."

Her announcement was met with loud groans. But to Christy, it was a sweeter sound than all the applause in the world.

About the Author

Catherine Marshall

With *Christy*, Catherine Marshall LeSourd (1914–1983) created one of the world's most widely read and best-loved classics. Published in 1967, the book spent 39 weeks on the New York Times bestseller list. With an estimated 30 million Americans having read it, *Christy* is now approaching its 90th printing and has sold more than eight million copies. Although a novel, *Christy* is in fact a thinly-veiled biography of Catherine's mother, Leonora Wood.

Catherine Marshall LeSourd also authored *A Man Called Peter*, which has sold more than four million copies. It is an American bestseller, portraying the love between a dynamic man and his God, and the tender, romantic love between a man and the girl he married.

Another one of Catherine's books is *Julie*, a powerful, sweeping novel of love and adventure, courage and commitment, tragedy and triumph, in a Pennsylvania town during the Great Depression. Catherine also authored many other devotional books of encouragement.

THE CHRISTY® FICTION SERIES

You'll want to read them all!

Based upon Catherine Marshall's international bestseller *Christy*®, this new series contains expanded adventures filled with romance, intrigue, and excitement.

#1—The Bridge to Cutter Gap
Nineteen-year-old Christy leaves her family to teach at a mission school in the Great Smoky Mountains. On the other side of an icy bridge lie excitement, adventure, and maybe even the man of her dreams . . . but can she survive a life-and-death struggle when she falls into the rushing waters below? (ISBN 0-8499-3686-1)

#2—Silent Superstitions
Christy's students are suddenly afraid to come to school. Is what Granny O'Teale says true? Is their teacher cursed? Will the children's fears and the adults' superstitions force Christy to abandon her dreams and return to North Carolina? (ISBN 0-8499-3687-X)

#3—The Angry Intruder
Someone wants Christy to leave Cutter Gap, and they'll stop at nothing. Mysterious pranks soon turn dangerous. Could a student be the culprit? When Christy confronts the late-night intruder, will it be a face she knows? (ISBN 0-8499-3688-8)

#4—Midnight Rescue
The mission's black stallion, Prince, has vanished, and so has Christy's student Ruby Mae. Christy must brave the guns of angry moonshiners to bring them home. Will her faith in God see her through her darkest night? (ISBN 0-8499-3689-6)

#5—The Proposal
Christy should be thrilled when David Grantland, the handsome minister, proposes marriage, but her feelings of excitement are mixed with confusion and uncertainty. Several untimely interruptions delay her answer to David's proposal. Then a terrible riding accident and blindness threaten all of Christy's dreams for the future. (ISBN 0-8499-3918-6)

#6—Christy's Choice
When Christy is offered a chance to teach in her hometown, she faces a difficult decision. Will her train ride back to Cutter Gap be a journey home or a last farewell? In a moment of terror and danger, Christy must decide where her future lies.
(ISBN 0-8499-3919-4)

#7—The Princess Club
When Ruby Mae, Bessie, and Clara discover gold at Cutter Gap, they form an exclusive organization, "The Princess Club." Christy watches in dismay as her classroom—and her community—are torn apart by greed, envy, and an understanding of what true wealth really means. (ISBN 0-8499-3958-5)

#8—Family Secrets
Bob Allen and many of the residents of Cutter Gap are upset when a black family, the Washingtons, moves in near the Allens' property. When a series of threatening incidents befall the Washingtons, Christy steps in to help. But it's a clue in the Washingtons' family Bible that may hold the real key to peace and acceptance. (ISBN 0-8499-3959-3)

#9—Mountain Madness
When Christy travels alone to a nearby mountain, she vows to discover the truth behind the terrifying

legend of a strange mountain creature. But what she finds at first seems worse than she ever imagined! (ISBN 0-8499-3960-7)

#10—Stage Fright

As Christy's students are preparing for a school play, she reveals her dream to act on stage herself. Little does she know that Doctor MacNeill's aunt is the artistic director of the Knoxville theater. Before long, just as Christy is about to debut on stage, several mysterious incidents threaten both her dreams and her pride! (ISBN 0-8499-3961-5)

An Excerpt
from

Mountain Madness

Book Nine in the Christy® Fiction Series

When Christy travels to nearby Boggin Mountain alone, she vows to discover the truth behind the terrifying legend of a strange mountain creature.

Boggin Mountain loomed above her. Somewhere in the forest, a branch cracked. Trees rustled. Thunder grumbled, a little closer this time.

Christy forced a grim smile. It suddenly occurred to her that when Clara had asked what she was afraid of, maybe Christy had left something out. Perhaps she should have added hiking alone through a dark, rainy forest, full of unfamiliar, creepy noises.

Christy picked up her pace. The last thing she wanted was to get caught in a forest during a lightning storm.

Suddenly, her shoe caught on a tree root. Christy tripped, crying out in surprise. She landed on her knees in a puddle.

"Oh, no," she moaned. "My skirt!"

As she struggled to get up, she heard footsteps nearing. They were coming from the direction of Boggin Mountain.

"Who's there?" Christy called. Her voice was just a thin whisper in the vast forest.

No answer. Nothing.

Still, Christy was certain she could feel the presence of another living thing close at hand.

Her breath caught in her throat. She could hear someone else—or something—breathing low and steadily.

It was watching her, whatever it was that was hidden in the dark, endless forest.

Christy didn't move. She seemed to have forgotten how to move. She peered into the shadows. A branch cracked to her right.

She looked, and then she saw it.

It was hideous. Monstrous. Its eyes glowed like an animal of the night.

It was the Boggin.